Death On

Duchess Street

Nanci M. Pattenden, PLCGS

DEATH ON DUCHESS STREET

Published by Murder Does Pay, Ink

Ontario, Canada

www.murderdoespayink.ca

ISBN 978-0-9918979-7-1

ACKNOWLEDGMENTS

Kudos to Infinite Pathways for their speedy and thorough editing and to Christopher Watts for his never ending talent with the graphics

THANK YOU

It's July, it's hot, it's stormy…and it's 1874. Detective Hodgins must close in on the perpetrator of a vicious murder in the time of buggy rides—not police cruisers—a fact that ramps up the suspense. Author Nanci M. Pattenden offers a masterful new voice in Victorian mystery!

Cynthia St-Pierre, co-author of A Purse to Die For

The era is a fantastic backdrop for such a heinous crime at a time when even the cops can be as bad as the criminals. Book 2 in the Detective Hodgins Victorian Mysteries series does not disappoint!

M.J. Moores, Infinite Pathways Press

I hope you enjoy *Death on Duchess Street*.
Please consider leaving a review at Goodreads
or your retailer of choice.
Sincerely,
Nanci M. Pattenden

Detective Hodgins Victorian Murder Mysteries

Body in the Harbour

Death on Duchess Street

Also available free on Kobo

End of the Line, A Short Story

CHAPTER 1

"Don't you worry Mr. Nolan. I'll take good care of Olivia." Flossie looked across the street at the auburn-haired girl standing on the porch of the two-storey clap-board dwelling, three houses down. "Such a pretty thing, and so polite. Won't be any bother at all."

Kendall Nolan followed Flossie's gaze and smiled. "She's growing up so fast. Won't be long now before she's married with a family of her own. I wish her mother was alive to see how Olivia turned out. Ruth would be so proud of her."

His smile faded slightly as he thought of his wife, her death still fresh in his mind even though it had been over a year since she succumbed to the consumption.

Flossie reached out to touch his arm, but caught herself in time. Even though he was far from wealthy, Kendall Nolan was a respected businessman. *She* ran a boarding house. It would be highly improper for someone of her standing to make such an intimate gesture.

Kendall turned back to Flossie as she quickly brushed

a few small strands of hair back in place, in an attempt to disguise her near error in judgement.

A gust of wind kicked up and dragged a small branch part-way across the road. Kendall grabbed his hat just as the wind caught it. Flossie fought with her dress as it wrapped around her legs.

"My goodness," Flossie said. "I thought the storm was over. I don't think these old trees can stand up against another one so soon."

"I see one of the shutters has come loose on the McGregor home," Kendall said as he pointed to the house across the road. "There it goes."

The shutter came off in the wind and crashed to the ground, crushing the Hydrangea bush.

"I hope my home is still standing when I get back. As I told you yesterday, I'll only be gone for the night. I'll be back late tomorrow morning. I'm sure Olivia will be fine, but I feel much better making this trip knowing there's someone in the house with her overnight. I didn't realize how much I relied on my sister since Ruth's death. She was such a big help."

"Why isn't she isn't able to come this time, if you don't mind me asking?" Flossie said.

"She passed early in June."

"Oh, I'm sorry for your loss."

"The past eighteen months have been dreadful for me and Olivia. First Ruth, then Penelope." Kendall got a far-away look in his eyes. "Dreadful year."

They stood silently for a moment. The air felt heavy after the storm despite the lingering wind. He could hear drops of water falling from the trees onto the rooftop as the wind moved through the branches. Kendall pulled a hanky from his pocket and wiped the sweat from his brow. He shook his head, clearing his thoughts.

"There's been so much going on in the neighbourhood lately I'm rather uncomfortable leaving Olivia alone."

Flossie nodded in agreement. "I can't believe how the area has changed in the last little while. I was shocked to hear Miss Gurney was arrested for stealing. Her father's out of work; it must be difficult feeding all those children. Still, that's no reason to break into a neighbour's home."

"That's not what's disturbing me. It's that missing woman around the corner on George Street, and that man, a painter I believe, murdered in his home only one block south, on Duke. I've been seriously thinking about moving, but you've seen how long the house beside me has sat vacant. No one wants to live here anymore." Kendall turned to Flossie. "Forgive me, Miss O'Hara. I did not intend to bring up such dreadful things. I do appreciate your help with my daughter."

Flossie blushed at his comment. Even though she was not upper class, he still treated her as a lady.

He tipped his hat, turned, and crossed the muddy road. Kendall looked at his daughter, not paying any attention to where he stepped. Halfway across the road his left foot hit the edge of a puddle, a remnant from the storm the day before.

Olivia moved off the porch and waited for him beside the hired cab. She laughed as her father approached.

"What's so funny young lady?"

Olivia pointed at his pant leg and continued giggling. The bottom edge of Kendall's white linen trousers had turned dark from the muddy water.

"Oh well," Kendall said. "It's too late to change now. It won't stay wet long in this heat. I'll brush off the dried mud before the train reaches Coboconk." He opened his arms and Olivia stepped closer to give him a hug.

"I'll miss you Papa. Have a safe trip and don't worry a bit about me. I'll be fine. I am sixteen you know. A grown woman. Well, almost." She rose up on her toes and gave her father a kiss on the cheek.

"Now you mind Miss O'Hara tonight. I don't want to come home and find you've been too much work for her," he joked. His mind drifted back to his conversation with

Flossie about the problems in the neighbourhood lately; his mood turned serious. "Make sure you keep the doors locked."

He kissed her on the top of her head and gently tugged on one of the ringlets that rested on her shoulder before climbing into the hansom cab and settling beside the carpet bag that Olivia had already placed on the seat. The driver gave a sharp snap on the reins, and the matching pair of reddish-brown Bay's picked up their hooves, pulling the cab away from the curb.

Olivia watched as her father travelled across Duchess Street, turned south on George, and disappeared from sight. She raised her skirts, and ran up the road to the boarding house, dodging the small rain puddles and deposits left by the horses.

Olivia was fond of her deceased aunt, but was looking forward to spending time with Miss O'Hara. Aunt Ruth always smelled of ointment and liniments. Miss O'Hara smelled of lavender and roses, just as her mother once did.

"What time will you be over, Miss O'Hara? I can make dinner for you. Father says I'm a very good cook."

"I'd love to join you for dinner Olivia, but I have two boarders and need to prepare their meal. Do you remember Mr. Webster? He stays with me quite often. Last time he mentioned that he spoke to you several times.

He's here on business again. Would you like to come across and join us for dinner? I'm sure he would be happy to see you."

Olivia frowned slightly at the mention of Mr. Webster. She remembered the first time she met him and all the attention the young man lavished on her.

"Yes, I remember him."

"My other guest is an older lady. She speaks of her grand-daughter all the time and how much she enjoys visiting her. I believe her grand-daughter is just about your age. I'm positive a visit from you would be most welcome, and she always has sweets in her purse. She mentioned not being able to see her family tonight so she will quite likely be a little sad this evening. It will be just like a little party. Wouldn't that be more fun than eating alone? We can walk over to your house afterwards."

"Yes, that would be nice. I baked apple pies first thing this morning. I can bring one over, if that would be all right."

Flossie brushed Olivia's wind-blown hair away from the girl's face and laughed. "Yes, that would be delightful. What about lunch? Your father didn't mention what you would be doing during the day. You won't be alone, will you?"

"No Miss. I'm going over to Sally's. Her mother is

packing a basket and we're having a picnic in the park with Lucy and Betsy - if it doesn't rain again and spoil things."

"Come over around five o'clock then, and you can help set the table. I have lots of work to do, so you run along. I'm sure you and your friends will have lots of fun now that school is over."

Olivia said goodbye and ran back across the street.

Flossie stood on her lawn for a minute looking around the neighbourhood. It had changed so much since she took over the boarding house. She grew up in the area and remembered how everyone had taken pride in their homes.

The Nolan house was well maintained and had been repainted the previous summer. It was still a lovely shade of light blue, and made the surrounding homes look dingy.

The vacant house beside it looked tired and lonely. The overgrown lawn was almost a foot high, and the flower garden around the porch had more weeds than flowers.

She turned and looked at her boarding house. From a distance it appeared well maintained, but the white paint around the windows peeled, and the railing on the porch steps leaned outward, as though trying to get away.

Flossie sighed. "At least the lace curtains look nice," she said to the squirrel busy burying an acorn in the lawn. It scampered away as she bustled towards the front door.

CHAPTER 2

Kendall paid the driver, picked up his bag, and made his way up the short walk to the porch.

"Olivia, I'm home. Olivia?"

He noticed the inside door ajar. Seeing his next door neighbour sweeping her porch, he called over, "Mrs. Green, have you seen Olivia this morning? I thought for sure she'd be here to meet me when I arrived."

"No, Mr. Nolan. I haven't seen her since yesterday. She went across to Miss O'Hara's at dinner time, and I haven't seen her since. Maybe she stayed overnight."

"Thank you. I'll go over shortly and check."

As he reached for the handle on the screen door he turned and looked toward the boarding house. Someone watched him from behind the front curtain. He waved, but the drape quickly closed.

Opening the door, he took a few steps in and dropped his bag on the floor beside the umbrella stand. Kendall removed his suit jacket as he went into the drawing room.

He stopped. The jacket dropped to the floor.

"Oh dear God. Olivia? Olivia?"

The sofa lay on its side, and some of Ruth's delicate figurines were scattered in pieces across the floor. He remembered the local girl who had been arrested for theft *I've been burgled.*

He backed out and hurried to the dining room to check if the silver was still there. Again, his eyes were drawn to the overturned chairs, then to the walls splattered with red spots and streaks. One small, bare foot stuck out from beneath a chair.

"Olivia!"

He ran to where she lay on the floor, throwing the chair off her limp body.

"No! Not my little angel."

He dropped to his knees beside her. Cradling her head in his lap, he called her name over and over.

His white linen suit soaked up his daughter's blood. The deep crimson formed a halo around his 'little angel's' head.

"Olivia. My dear God. Olivia."

Kendall gently touched her cheek. She was no longer warm and soft. He jerked his hand away in shock, her beautiful porcelain skin now cold and sallow.

"Mr. Nolan? Is everything all right?"

Kendall's voice had carried through the house. Alice

Green could hear his frantic calls as she hurried across the lawn to his porch.

"Mr. Nolan?"

She opened the screen door and stepped in, following his voice. When she reached the dining room, she stopped.

Backing away from the entry, she turned and ran.

"Help, help. Oh Lord. Someone please help."

Several neighbours came out to the street to see what the commotion was. Alice's husband, Sam, turned the corner from George Street, heading home for lunch as he did every work day.

"Sam! Find the constable," she yelled. "Quick. Something bad has happened to Olivia."

Her body shook as she wrung her hands, trying to comprehend the horrific scene in the Nolan house. Without waiting to find out what exactly was wrong, Sam ran back the way he'd come.

Constable Barnes was making his rounds. Sam ran up to him and grabbed his arm.

"Constable, quickly. Something terrible has happened. Hurry, please. On Duchess Street."

Mrs. McGregor had come out of her house and ran over to Mrs. Green to try and calm her.

"Whatever is the matter Alice?" she asked. "Why did you send for the constable?"

Alice looked over at the Nolan house. "Oh Catharine," she sobbed. "Olivia . . . blood everywhere . . . Mr. Nolan . . . horrible, so horrible." Catharine put her arm around Alice, and guided her to the shade of the old oak that stood between the Green and Nolan properties.

Constable Barnes came running down the street, with Sam several feet behind. Barnes stopped beside the oak as Sam collapsed on the ground by Alice and Catherine, his face red, and his breathing laboured.

Alice pointed to the Nolan home. Barnes ran across the lawn, up the porch, and inside.

In less than a minute he came back out, blowing his whistle to alert the other policemen in the area. Barnes dashed around the side of the house, placed one hand on the wall for support, bent over and threw up. He pulled a hanky from his pocket, wiped his mouth and took a deep breath.

"Oh Lord, what monster did that?" he muttered. "Keep your head Henry," he told himself. "Look at the scene, not that poor innocent child."

He turned around to see if anyone noticed him vomiting and talking to himself. He straightened his uniform jacket and pushed his helmet into place before going back inside to the dining room.

"Mr. Nolan. There's nothing you can do for her.

Please, you have to leave the house. We need to investigate so we can figure out what happened."

"Miss O'Hara," Kendall whispered. "Miss O'Hara."

"What's that, Sir?" Barnes asked. "Who's Miss O'Hara?"

"Runs the boarding house . . . up the street," Kendall sputtered. "Supposed to stay . . . with Olivia . . . last night. Where is she?" He looked up at Constable Barnes. "Where is she?" he whispered. Kendall clutched his daughter tighter. "You don't think . . . ?"

The constable glanced at Olivia's body. Barnes could taste the bile rising and burning in his throat. He turned away, pretending to look around the room.

The coppery smell was overpowering as his hyperosmia increased his sense of smell. He was glad of it around food, but it was not a condition that benefitted a police officer. His stomach settled and he turned back to Nolan.

"We have to leave now, Sir. Please. We'll check the rest of the house."

Barnes put his hand on Kendall's shoulder and Kendall reluctantly released his hold on Olivia. He gently laid her head on the hard wooden floor. Blood seeped into the crevices. A few drops fell from his shirt cuff when he grabbed the table to steady himself as he stood.

Barnes swallowed hard and took another deep breath as he led Kendall out to the porch. When Alice saw Kendall's blood-stained suit, she fainted. Sam barely had time to grab her before her oversized frame hit the ground. Catharine removed her apron and fanned her friend's face.

Two officers finally arrived in response to Barnes' earlier whistle blows. He waved them over.

"Smith, hurry up to the station and fetch Detective Hodgins." Barnes turned to the other constable and pointed to the crowd that was gathering. "Keep those people away from the house. Stand guard at the porch. I don't want anyone going in and disturbing things."

Once Barnes was satisfied the house was secure he went over to Mrs. McGregor.

"Could you take Mr. Nolan over to your house? He's in shock and shouldn't be left alone. I'll send for a doctor to check on him as soon as I can."

Catharine bellowed at her husband, "Put the kettle on Franklin! Make yourself useful. Poor man needs a cuppa tea."

She led Kendall to a chair on her front porch, then hurried into the house. She returned a moment later with an old blanket and a cup of hot tea. "Added a wee dram to it. For medicinal purposes," she told Kendall as she placed the blanket around his shoulders. Satisfied he was comfortable, she sat in the chair beside him to watch the goings on. Reaching into her apron pocket, she pulled out a small bottle, took a swig, and leaned forward, straining to hear what the constable was asking Alice Green.

Barnes pulled his notebook out of his pocket and leaned against the old oak tree.

"Could I have your name please?"

"Mrs. Green. Alice," she whispered as she leaned against her husband.

"Mrs. Green, can you tell me what happened?"

She stared at the Nolan house. "Yelling."

"Who was yelling, ma'am?"

"Horrible. Blood everywhere."

"Who was yelling Mrs. Green? Was it the girl?"

Mrs. Green continued to stare at the house, now wringing her skirts.

"Mrs. Green?" Barnes reached out and touched her arm. She jumped.

"Mrs. Green, you said you heard yelling. Was it the girl?

"No. Him. *Olivia, Olivia.* Said her name over and over."

Alice's husband Sam had heard enough

"No more questions Constable. Can't you see my wife

is in no condition to continue?" He helped her up off the grass and took her into the house.

Barnes turned the page of his notebook and started to interview the residents who had come out of their homes.

Until they had heard Alice screaming, no one knew anything was wrong. Barnes turned towards the boarding house to inquire about Miss O'Hara when he saw Detective Hodgins run around the corner.

"Detective, thank God you're here." Barnes told Hodgins what had happened and led him into the house. The constable hesitated just inside the front door and pointed down the hall to the dining room.

"She's in there, Sir. It's pretty gruesome."

Hodgins took in the surroundings as Barnes spoke.

"Bloody walls? Must have been quite the fight. Amazing how much blood we have inside our bodies. Often looks like more than it actually is."

He turned and noticed how pale Barnes had become.

"Unfortunately you'll get use to it. Well, maybe not used to it, but you'll learn to cope. Only way to get things done."

He pulled out his weathered notebook, identical to the one the Constable had started using, and made a few notes.

"It looks like it may have started in the drawing

room," Hodgins said. He walked down the hall, with Barnes following close behind. "Nothing is disturbed here by the door, but things have been broken in there. She must have run down that side of the hall. See there? The portrait on the wall is crooked, yet nothing on the opposite side of the hall is out of place." Barnes walked past the Detective and Hodgins reached out and grabbed Barnes by the arm.

"Watch where you step Constable. There's bloody footprints leading out the door. Could belong to the killer."

"No, Sir," Barnes said. "The hall was clean when I came in. I believe they belong to Mr. Nolan. He was cradling his daughter's body and soaked up a considerable amount of her blood."

"Just where is Nolan?"

"I asked one of the neighbours to watch him. They're on the front porch two over. He's pretty shaken up, as you can well imagine."

"Afternoon gentlemen," a voice said behind them.

They turned as Dr. McKenzie entered through the front door. "I've been told there's a body here."

"In here." Barnes took a calming breath and lead McKenzie inside the dining room.

McKenzie knelt beside Olivia and reached to start his

examination.

"One moment Doctor," Hodgins said. "Constable, is this how you found the room? Has anything been touched or moved?"

"Mr. Nolan moved his daughter when he took her in his arms. I don't know if he moved anything else. Nothing has been disturbed since I arrived."

Hodgins made a quick sketch of the room, then allowed McKenzie to proceed.

"Such a pretty little thing," McKenzie said. "Why would anyone want to harm this wee lassie?"

"That's what I plan on finding out," Hodgins replied.

CHAPTER 3

Hodgins waved his hand, motioning Barnes to follow him into the front hall.

"There's muddy footprints everywhere. I suppose they're courtesy of you as well?"

"No, Sir." Barnes placed his foot beside one of the muddy prints. "Bit smaller small than mine. And I do believe everyone else who came in is bigger than me, 'cept Mrs. Green, but I don't believe she tracked any mud in with her." He looked sheepish and half smiled. "Guess I was thinkin' about the girl and didn't notice them."

"What else do you see?"

Barnes looked around. "Well, as you said, there's mud everywhere."

"Mud and dirt. It's partly dried up so it was left awhile ago."

"Maybe by the guy what killed that poor child," Barnes exclaimed. He looked around again. "The stairs. There's more on the stairs." He walked to the foot of the staircase and pointed up. "They go all the way to the top."

Hodgins started up the staircase, keeping close to the wall, careful not to disturb the crime scene. Barnes followed, mimicking Hodgins' actions. Some of the steps had a print, others just globs of semi-dry mud. About half way up Hodgins stopped and knelt down.

"Look here. The prints only go down. They're far too large to belong to the child. Besides, how would her feet get muddy?" Hodgins cocked his head. "How did someone get upstairs during a rain storm without leaving prints?"

He stood and continued to the top. The prints were spaced farther apart than normal. "Looks like he was running. Probably chasing the girl."

"Olivia," Barnes whispered.

"What was that?"

"Olivia. The girl's name is Olivia."

Hodgins turned to face Barnes. The young constable still seemed pale despite the deep tan covering his face.

"You all right lad?"

"She's so young. Same age as my sister. Don't seem fair."

Hodgins sighed. "No, it's not fair. That's why we're here. To make sure someone pays for what they did to the girl. To *Olivia*."

They followed the mud down the narrow hall and into

one of the bedrooms.

"Olivia's room," Barnes said peeking around Hodgins.

Hodgins nodded in agreement.

A single shelf on the far wall was lined with dolls of various sizes, with a ratty looking stuffed cat sitting in the centre. None were the same quality as the ones his mother-in-law had purchased for his daughter Sara, but most were well cared for.

One of the dolls had a crack running from the corner of her eye all the way down to her chin, and her once rosy-red cheeks were barely noticeable. Another was missing a shoe. A picture of Olivia's bare foot splattered with blood crossed through his mind. He concentrated on the task at hand and pushed the image to the side.

He focused on the room. The bed sheets and matching curtains were a faded pink. The dressing table had one bottle of lilac toilet-water, a couple of small silver hair combs, a hand mirror, and matching brush, all arranged neatly on a piece of frosted glass. A fan was spread open on one side of it, ribbons of all colours sat on the other side. The room was part child, part young woman.

Barnes tapped Hodgins' shoulder and said, "The window."

Hodgins turned his head and noticed the curtains

fluttering. "It's open." He glanced down at the floor below the window. "More mud. He must have come in through this window. Did anyone check out back?"

"Don't know. No one said, so I guess not." Barnes paused a moment. "I'll go 'round back."

Hodgins listened to Barnes' boots echo off the wooden floor as he went down the empty hall and staircase, followed by a door slam.

The detective walked to the window, drew back the curtains and stuck his head out, watching for Barnes to come around the corner of the house. A ladder rested on the ground not far from the back wall of the house.

"Down there," Hodgins yelled, pointing to the ground below the window. "Anything?

Barnes walked back and forth, stepping over the ladder. The grass went right up to the back wall. There were a few depressions where someone might have stood, but no foot prints.

"Looks like the ladder was up against the house," Barnes hollered up. "There are two holes where it was set." He looked at the ladder. "Holes are about the right distance apart. It probably fell when he climbed inside."

"Stay put. I'm coming down."

Hodgins pulled his head in and took another look around the room. The crumpled sheets, half on the floor, spoke to him. She must have fled down the stairs and tried to hid in the drawing room, killer running after her. There was no blood in the room, so she probably heard him when the ladder hit the sill or when he opened the window. Going back down, he took another look at the crooked pictures on the wall, half way down the hall. The remaining pictures were still straight. *Probably caught up with her here.*

Hodgins hesitated at the bottom of the stairs. Dr. McKenzie and one of the constables were preparing Olivia's body for transport to the morgue. The young girl's body had been placed on a stretcher. Hodgins watched as Dr. McKenzie unfolded a clean white sheet. The constable took one end and they laid it over her still frame. The sheet flapped out like the wings of an angel, preparing to take Olivia to Heaven.

Hodgins wanted to speak with McKenzie, but decided it could wait. Instead he went out the front door, around the house, and joined Barnes in the back yard.

"Whoever did this came prepared," Hodgins surmised. "Either he brought the ladder with him or knew where to find one. Maybe one of the neighbours knows if the ladder belongs to Nolan. Can't imagine the bloke carried a ladder that size around un-noticed. It's not likely anyone was out in that storm, and it was extra dark with the thick cloud cover. I doubt anyone would have seen much. A herd of elephants could have stood in the yard and no one would have seen them."

"The killer could have come over from that empty house there, or up the laneway," Barnes said.

Hodgins smiled. "You're getting to be quite observant, lad. Might as well check the laneway. Who knows, we may get lucky and find something useful."

They walked over to the gap in the fence that separated the lane from Nolan's yard.

"Wonder how long that's been there?" Barnes asked.

Hodgins opened his notebook and jotted a few words. "Another question for Nolan."

He squeezed through the fence, and leaned against it to give Barnes some room.

"Watch out --"

"Ewwww."

". . . for the mud," Hodgins finished.

The dirt laneway had become a river of brown sludge. It sloped slightly so much of the rain ran down from the road. It was anything but dry.

"Don't know about you, but I don't think I want to check the lane today," Hodgins said.

"Won't get no argument from me, Sir." Barnes tried to retreat, but the four inch thick mud had a stranglehold on the constable's boots.

Hodgins laughed and held out his arm. "Grab hold and I'll pull."

Barnes twisted his body and reached back. They grabbed each other just below the elbow and Hodgins tugged. On the fourth pull one foot was released with a loud squelch.

Once Barnes had one foot on solid ground by the fence, his other foot followed with only a little resistance. He went through the fence back into the yard, Hodgins close behind, still chuckling.

"Can't have one of our constables looking like that," Hodgins said. "Better trot off home and put on a clean pair of trousers. And clean the muck off your boots. I'll see if McKenzie has finished up. Meet me back at the station. Get going now. Sharpish."

CHAPTER 4

Friday morning Detective Hodgins sat re-reading the notes Barnes had given him. He tossed them down on the desk and walked to his office door. Looking around the station house he spotted the constable coming from the back room, chatting with one of the men.

"Barnes!" he hollered.

Constable Barnes didn't need to turn around to know who wanted him. The officer he was with snickered.

"Whatcha mess up now, Henry?" he asked. Barnes shrugged and hustled over to the waiting detective.

"Yes, Sir?"

Hodgins motioned to the chair in front of his desk. "Don't look so worried. I just want to go over your notes."

Barnes sat down and a sigh of relief escaped his mouth.

Hodgins smiled and sat on the edge of his desk. He reached back and picked up the notes on Olivia Nolan.

"Your note taking is impressive. Much improved since the Walker case.

Barnes' face turned a deep crimson. "I've been trying real hard, Sir. And it's never happened again," he stammered.

"Relax, Constable. You're not in trouble. I'm just saying you've come a long way, and in such a short time." He shook his head; the smile quickly fell from his face. "It's unbelievable someone could do that to an innocent child. I feel for her father. My Sara is several years younger, and I can't image finding her like that. It's too horrible to even think about."

He picked up a small silver frame that held a cabinet-card photograph of his wife and daughter. Hodgins moved around his desk and put the frame back in place before dropping into his chair. "I've got the coroner's report. McKenzie was his usual thorough self." He opened a folder and picked up a sheet of paper. "Seems the girl was beaten about the head. There were bits of wood in her hair and skin. That bastard even cut her throat." His voice wavered.

Hodgins hesitated for a moment. "She had bruises on her arms. Legs too. I suspect he tried to have his way with her. Fortunately McKenzie says the girl was not interfered with." He put the paper back inside the folder and slammed it down on his desk.

Neither man spoke for several minutes.

"We'll find him, Sir," Barnes said. "Someone must've heard something. With all the overturned furniture and broken figurines, he must've made quite some noise."

Hodgins nodded. "Yes, I'm sure she likely screamed too. It's summer, and it's been hotter than blazes. People may have had their windows open even a tiny bit during the rain, just for the breeze. I find it hard to believe none of the neighbours heard a sound. The thunder wasn't constant. We'll have to talk to them again. See if they've remembered anything now they've had time to mull the events of the evening over. Grab your notebook."

* * *

The men stood in front of the Nolan home. "Where is Mr. Nolan staying?" Hodgins asked.

"Two doors over, with the McGregor's," Barnes said.

Hodgins looked at the puddles scattered around the road. "Sure has been a lot of rain these past few days. Looks like we caught a break with the weather today. Maybe the sun will put these people in a better mood."

He took in the layout of the neighbouring houses. "She was killed on the thirteenth, Monday night, or possibly very early Tuesday morning. The houses aren't that far apart. Why didn't someone hear her?" He shook his head in disbelief. "Has the lady who stayed with Miss Nolan said anything yet?"

Barnes flipped through his notebook. "Miss O'Hara. She was supposed to have stayed with Olivia while Mr. Nolan was away. Constable Smith went over to her boarding house yesterday, but she wouldn't tell him anything. She won't give a statement. Won't talk about it to anyone."

"We'll see about that. I'll pay her a visit while you see if the neighbours have any more information."

Hodgins crossed the road and walked toward the boarding house. He spotted a woman out back as he approached. He reached over the gate in the picket fence, lifted the latch and stopped short.

The gate wouldn't budge.

He rattled it a few times then gave it a good swift kick. It swung open, but didn't hang straight. The bottom hinge had come off. Hodgins looked around to see if anyone witnessed him damage it.

The street was empty.

Feeling guilty, he made a mental note to have one of the lads repair it. He left it open and went around the house to the back garden. "Miss O'Hara?"

The woman dropped her basket of vegetables and turned. "Gracious, you gave me a start."

Hodgins smiled when she turned. She bore a slight resemblance to his wife. Same Irish complexion and red

28

hair. Miss O'Hara was several years younger though. "Sorry ma'am. I'm Detective Hodgins. I need to speak with you about Miss Nolan."

"Miss Nolan? Olivia? I didn't see a thing. I'm afraid there's nothing I can tell you. Now if you'll excuse me, I'm terribly busy." Flossie reached down, righted the basket and picked up the beets and carrots that had tumbled out.

"I must insist Miss O'Hara. We speak now or down at the station."

Flossie's shoulders dropped and she let out a tiny sigh. She pointed at a wooden bench under a thirty foot Maple.

"We can sit over there. I don't want my guests disturbed."

Hodgins nodded and moved towards the bench. Flossie left the basket on the ground and followed. Hodgins waited until she was settled before he sat. He removed his hat, placed it on the bench between them, and pulled his notebook and pencil out of his pocket.

"According to Mr. Nolan, you stayed overnight in the house with his daughter. Several things had been broken, the furniture was overturned, and an obvious struggle had taken place. I find it difficult to believe you heard nothing."

Flossie reached down beside the bench and pinched a dead flower from a Cleome.

"Miss O'Hara? Why didn't you get help?"

She mumbled something that Hodgins couldn't quite hear. "You'll have to speak up."

"I said I wasn't there." She dropped her head to her hands and cried. "Lord forgive me, I wasn't there." She pulled a lace handkerchief from her sleeve and patted her eyes.

Hodgins made a few notes, then asked, "Why weren't you there? Start from the beginning. Take your time." He sat with his pencil poised, waiting.

CHAPTER 5

Barnes watched Hodgins disappear behind the boarding house, then looked around at the surrounding houses, trying to decide where to go first. Empty house to the west of Nolan's, the Green's house to the east beside the mud-filled lane. Mrs. Green had found Kendall cradling Olivia's body, and had become hysterical when he tried to interview her that day. Mr. Green was none too pleased with him. They could wait.

Next was the McGregor home. Kendall Nolan was staying there until the police permitted him return to his own home. *Nope, don't want to disturb him just yet.* He turned back to the empty house. *Good place to hide.* Decision made, he cut across the grass and circled the house, looking for a way in.

The ground was wet and muddy from the intermittent storms and rain over the previous three days. The tall grass and weeds slapped against Barnes' trousers, quickly soaking him to the skin. He reached down and tried to pull the wet cloth away from his legs. As he twisted to reach the back of his pants leg, he noticed several muddy footprints leading to and from the Nolan yard.

Pulling his notebook out he tried to sketch the prints just the way Hodgins always did. Barnes didn't understand why the detective insisted on sketching out everything. They made copious notes on every case, but that was never enough for Hodgins. Knowing that Hodgins would want to check this himself, he ran up the street to the boarding house. He paused at the broken gate then continued around back, stopping at the edge of the garden.

"Pardon, Sir. Sorry to interrupt, but I've found something you'll want to see."

Hodgins closed his notebook. "That's all right Barnes. I'm done here, for now." He reached for his hat as he stood. "I'll have more questions later," he said to Flossie. He tipped his hat and left with Barnes. As they passed though the gate, Hodgins asked Barnes to find someone to repair it.

"Don't ask," was the only reply to Barnes' puzzled look.

"Over there, Sir. Footprints. Could be from the killer."

Hodgins followed him through the path Barnes had made in the wet, trampled grass. As they made their way around to the back, Hodgins surveyed the grounds. He didn't notice when the young constable stopped.

"Yee-ouch," Barnes screamed as the detective's foot connected with his heel.

"What the blazes?"

"Sorry, Sir. The prints are right here. Didn't want to wreck them."

"Hmm. Right. Good thinking."

Hodgins looked at the Nolan house, then at the vacant one. He motioned towards the empty house. "May as well see where the prints came from."

He walked parallel to the footprints, with Barnes close behind, and stopped at the back porch steps, where the prints seemed to vanish.

"What now, Sir?" Barnes asked. "There aren't any more prints. Bugger could have come from any direction."

Hodgins shook his head. "Look closer, Constable." He pointed to the top of the steps. "The porch."

Barnes took a few steps forward and examined the area around the top of the steps. Shrugging his shoulders he said, "Nothing but a few swirls of mud."

Hodgins sighed. "Haven't you learned anything man? Notice the porch has sunk a little on the west side. You can see where the rain has been flowing across and off the west end of the porch. The swirls of mud are quite likely muddy footprints that were partially washed away by the running water. The rain would have cleaned any marks off the steps. I think he was hiding inside."

"Very smart, Sir. I see what you mean. I guess we need to obtain a search warrant then."

"Possibly. Find the owner. If he gives consent, then we don't need one." Barnes stood beside Hodgins, looking around. "Well, get on it, Constable. Haven't got all day."

Barnes nodded once, then headed off to search the records for the owner, while Hodgins walked up the steps of the house. He spotted a window at the east end of the porch and made his way down to it, stepping over a small branch that had come off a nearby tree. Some of the nails from the bottom board had come out and the window was partially exposed. He bent over to peer in, but with all the windows boarded up, no light was getting in except for a tiny sliver where the board had shifted. He could make out vague shapes, and thought it might be the kitchen, but wasn't really sure.

"Blast." He slammed his fist on the window sill, causing the un-nailed end of the board to slip a little more. He was tempted to pull the board the rest of the way off, but thought better of it. Didn't want anyone in the neighbourhood seeing him try to break in. He stormed off the porch, slipping on the bottom step.

"Damn."

He landed in the mud, and slipped again when he tried

to stand.

"Damn, damn, damn."

He managed to get back on his feet, and looked around to see if anyone witnessed his undignified descent.

Hodgins tried brushing off the thick, smelly mud, but just made it worse. He knew he couldn't examine the Nolan house or interview the neighbours looking as he did. With as much dignity as he could muster, he hurried home to change.

* * *

Hodgins went in the back door to avoid tracking mud through the house He was glad he had saved enough money to purchase a house of his own, he just wished it wasn't so close to his in-laws. A house in the country would have been ideal. *Maybe when I retire.* He could almost hear his mother-in-law scolding him for tracking mud into the house. His wife, Cordelia, was so much more easy going than her mother.

The door barely had time to close when he heard the clicking of nails on the hardwood floor. A dog raced across the kitchen and jumped up, placing two hairy brown paws on Hodgins' chest, it's weight causing him to take a step back.

The dog had grown considerably since bringing it home six months earlier as a present for his daughter's ninth birthday. It had transformed from a dirty, scrawny, timid mutt into a healthy, sturdy, extremely affectionate dog. *Hardly looks like the same creature that hung around the station house.* His hands automatically reached out and scratched behind Scraps' ears for a moment.

One of the sergeants had named the dog Scraps since that was what it had been eating for most of the first two years of its life. A lot of those scraps were courtesy of the men of the Toronto Constabulary, himself included.

Hodgins smiled as he remembered his stay in the hospital after the train explosion earlier in the year. Barnes had been speechless at his request to catch the dog, clean it up, and have Dr. McKenzie give it check up. His daughter and the dog had become inseparable ever since.

"Why are you home so early Papa?"

Startled by his daughter's sudden appearance, Hodgins pushed the dog away. Sara giggled when she saw his mud-covered suit. He glared at her, then smiled. He looked down at his clothing and started laughing too.

"I guess I do look quite the sight."

He removed his shoes and socks, placed them on the bumper of the pot belly stove, and walked across the kitchen. As he passed Sara, he ran a finger across his jacket and gently placed a drop of mud on the tip of her nose.

"Are you feeling better? Your colour seems much

improved. How's your throat?"

"Yes, Papa. Much better. Mama called the doctor this morning. He gave me some medicine. It tasted just awful, but it made my throat all better. Mama said I can go swimming in a few days."

He ruffled her hair. "As long as the doctor agrees."

Hodgins went up to his room, walked over to the dry sink, and poured water from the pitcher into the bowl. He removed his jacket, shirt and trousers then draped them over the arm of a small wooden chair. Cordelia came in while he was wetting the face cloth. She watched while he cleaned up, put on a fresh shirt and suit and ran a brush through his hair.

Cordelia looked from the dirty suit to her husband. "What have you been up to now?" she asked.

"Had a disagreement with a muddy step." He looked over at his soiled suit. "I don't think there was any damage, but maybe you can check it over. Might have caught it on something."

Cordelia walked over to the suit for a closer look. "I think I'll wait for it to dry before cleaning it. I'll examine it when I brush off the dried dirt. Do you have to go back to the station? It is rather late in the afternoon."

"Yes, I'm afraid so. I've sent Barnes out for information and I'd like to know what he finds. I'm sure I won't be long. I'll tell you all about it over supper."

He applied a small amount of wax to reshape his moustache, then went back downstairs with Cordelia. They found Sara sitting cross-legged on the kitchen floor, wiping the last of the mud from his shoes, Scraps lay curled up beside her.

He knelt down, kissed her cheek, put his shoes on, kissed his wife and then headed back to Station Number Four.

CHAPTER 6

Hodgins entered the station and immediately wished he could go back out. All the windows were open, but the stench of sweat hung in the air. He fought back the urge to leave and looked around for his constable.

"Barnes not around?" he asked no one in particular.

"Ain't seem 'im," replied someone behind him.

Recognizing the gruff voice of the desk Sergeant, Hodgins turned and addressed him. "Has he come in at all?"

The Sergeant shook his head. "Ain't seen him since he left with you earlier."

"Must still be looking for the owner of the vacant house," he mumbled. Turning, he walked into his office. As he sat down the station door closed with a bang.

All heads turned.

Barnes rushed across the room. Beads of sweat spotted his forehead. He stopped at Hodgins' office and leaned on the door frame, huffing and puffing from rushing in the heat.

Hodgins motioned to the chair in front of his desk and Barnes dropped into the seat.

"Might I be so bold as to remove my helmet, Sir?" Barnes asked.

Hodgins waved his hand, dismissing protocol. "By all means. What's got you all worked up? It's too blasted hot to be rushing around."

Barnes unfastened the chin strap, removed the helmet and placed it at the edge of Hodgins' desk. He removed a hanky from his pocket and wiped his face before speaking. The clean white hanky was quickly covered in dirt and grit from the roads, a few streaks still remaining on the constables' slightly sun-burned face.

"Sir, I discovered who owns the vacant house. You won't believe it." Barnes took a few deep breaths. "William Howland."

Hodgins tilted his head slightly. "Howland? That name sounds familiar."

"He's the new President of the Board of Trade, Sir. Purchased the house . . ." Barnes pulled his notebook out and flipped the pages. "Here it is. He bought it just a few months ago." He looked up at Hodgins. "Shall I make inquires with him?"

Hodgins shook his head. "No, I think I'll take care of that personally."

Barnes looked relieved. "Very good, Sir. To tell the truth, I'm not very comfortable talking to officials."

Hodgins smiled. "You'll get used to it eventually. Give it time. You've only been an officer for a short while. Board of Trade, eh? Wonder what he wants with a house in St. David's Ward? Not a district filled with the wealthy and connected."

"Maybe he plans to rent it. An investment like."

"Possibly. I seem to recall reading an article about him. I believe he wants to clean up the slums in the city. Could be he plans to take that challenge personally and purchased a house in a neighbourhood that's starting to get run down. Stop it in its tracks, so to speak."

Hodgins pulled out his pocket watch. "I think it best to leave the inquires until tomorrow, it's getting late and I don't want to interrupt his dinner. Write up a report on what you found and leave it on my desk. Speaking of dinner, I believe I'll head home and see what's waiting for me."

Both men rose from their chairs; Barnes headed towards his small table, Hodgins towards the front door.

"Oh Barnes," Hodgins said without stopping or turning around, "You might want to wipe the rest of the city off your face."

* * *

Hodgins stepped off the trolley car a few blocks from his house. The short walk before having his evening meal helped erase all thoughts of the day's crime.

Most of the houses he passed had beautiful gardens under the front windows. The fragrances along the way relaxed him and put him in a good mood by the time he walked through his front door.

His front door.

He enjoyed saying that after living with his in-laws for ten long years, but it had allowed him to put most of his paycheques into his savings account nonetheless.

Unfortunately they still weren't completely free of her parents. Even though he gave Cordelia an allowance for clothing and other women's things, her mother doted on her as though she was still a young, unmarried girl. She was twice as bad with Sara. While it was nice that his wife and daughter were dressed in the most fashionable clothing, it still put a dent in his pride.

He stopped on the sidewalk outside his house and smiled. They had only been there for a few weeks, but it felt like home. His smile faded as he looked at the property. The house had been vacant only a few months, but it was long enough that the lawn and gardens had suffered. He had a Saturday off soon, and planned on helping Cordelia as much as he could.

She had been busy buying up fabrics and sewing curtains, but most of the rooms remained sparsely furnished. Her parents insisted they take the bedroom sets with them, and he really didn't mind. They were quite nice and very well crafted.

They got a second hand table set for the kitchen, another for the dining room, along with a few other bits of furnishings from an acquaintance who was clearing out the house of his recently deceased, widowed mother. All very good quality and kept in immaculate condition.

All thoughts of his current case completely vanished and he let out a sigh of satisfaction before going inside. His movements echoed in the empty hallway, alerting the dog. Scraps came racing down the hall, nails clicking on the wooden floor. The dog tried to stop, but slid into Hodgins, knocking him off balance. He hit the floor with a thud, and Scraps pounced on top, trying to lick Hodgins' face.

He was used to Sara running to greet him, but he hadn't managed to figure out how to get inside without being bowled over by the new addition to the family. Both Cordelia and Sara came out of the kitchen to see what had happened. Sara started to giggle, then Delia. Hodgins stopped trying to push the dog away and scratched behind Scraps' ears instead.

"I hope a hall runner is on your list of purchases. The *top* of the list," he said to his wife. The dog had settled down enough for Hodgins to push him off and get up. "Just look at the scratches on the floor. Guess I'll have to add that to *my* list."

CHAPTER 7

The next morning Hodgins walked past Nolan's house and paused at the laneway running past the east side of the house. He took a few steps in and stopped. The lane was still muddy from the storm.

Not wanting to soil his trousers or get stuck like Barnes had, he stepped back and continued to the McGregor house. A shutter stuck out from under a hydrangea bush and a pile of twigs and small branches lay beside the front porch. He stopped to survey the neighbourhood.

There was more damage then he remembered. He figured the distraction of the murder was to blame for his lack of attention; he normally took in everything surrounding a crime scene. Several of the houses had debris on their front lawns. A large branch leaned against the porch roof a few house over.

He started up the walk to the McGregor's front porch when a gust of wind raced through the branches of the Oak. A branch that had been broken during the storm came free and bounced off Hodgins' shoulder, landing on the walk in front of him. Without missing a step, he scooped it up and deposited it on the debris pile McGregor had started, then climbed the porch steps.

As he raised his hand to knock, the front door opened. Mr. Nolan rushed out and plowed into him.

Hodgins grabbed the railing to avoid falling.

Nolan dropped the satchel he was carrying. It popped open and a few shirts tumbled out. Nolan's hair stuck out in all directions and his suit was covered in wrinkles. Hodgins guessed he had slept in it.

Taking a closer look at Nolan's face, he noticed his eyes were red and puffy. *Maybe he hadn't really slept at all.*

"You can't go back to your home. Not just yet." Hodgins said.

Nolan shook his head. "Not going home. I'm leaving town for a few days. Need to clear my head." He knelt down to stuff the shirts back into the satchel.

"Relatives?"

"Friend."

"I still have several questions for you that need to be answered."

Nolan pointed up the street. "My carriage is here. Have to catch the train."

"Where will you be staying? What's your friend's

name?"

"You can send a message care of the post office in Woodbridge." He stood and rushed to the curb, leaving Hodgins standing on the porch.

"Wot ya be wanting now?"

Hodgins jumped at the sound of the brusque voice behind him. Mr. McGregor stood in the doorway of his house. His thick accent suggesting he hadn't left Scotland that many years ago.

"Isnae a goot time ta be botherin' folk."

"I just needed to speak with Mr. Nolan, but it seems I'm too late. I may need to speak with you later." Hodgins tipped his hat and walked down the steps. The door slammed shut behind him.

He cut across the lawn and went next door to the Green's. Their property seemed untouched by the storm. *Maybe they just cleaned up quicker than McGregor.* It wasn't the best neighbourhood, but it wasn't the poorest either. Hodgins couldn't image leaving a shutter off his house. Lazy sot couldn't even be bothered to remove it from the front garden.

Hodgins knocked on the Green's front door. The scent of freshly baked peach pies wafted through the open windows. He didn't have long to wait before Mrs. Green appeared.

"Yes? What can I do for you?" She spoke softly and it looked as though she had been crying.

"I'm Detective Hodgins. I have a few questions regarding the death of Miss Nolan."

Mrs. Green reached into her apron pocket and removed a lacy hanky. She waved in front of her face a few times then started sobbing before burying her face in it.

"Oh, that poor child. Never seen such a thing in all my days." She wiped her eyes then began to wail.

Hodgins recalled reading about her in Barnes' report. He had thought Barnes was exaggerating, but clearly this was a very emotional and highly strung woman. Mr. Green came barrelling down the hall.

"What have you done to my wife? Be off with you." He put his arm around her shoulder and started to close the door.

"Wait," Hodgins said. He put his hand out to stop the door. "I have a few questions about the murder next door."

Mrs. Green wailed even louder, which Hodgins had thought impossible. He showed his badge.

"Might I have a word with you? Only take a few minutes."

"Well, I guess I can spare a few minutes. Let me take care of my wife first." He shut the door, leaving Hodgins to wait on the porch.

He was glad the rain was over. The past few weeks were the wettest Hodgins had seen for quite some time. A couple of days of heavy rain and strong winds followed by a few beautiful sunny days. The most recent rainfall had washed away the humidity. The sun was out and the air was fresh.

While he waited he looked over the garden running along the front of the house. It was immaculate. The steps were in the centre of the porch and the gardens on each side matched perfectly.

On either side of the steps was a well manicured deep red rose bush. Two more were at each corner of the house. Rows of gladiolus in all colours stood at the back of the garden against the house. When he first arrived he hadn't noticed that several of them were broken from the storm. Deep purple and yellow pansies filled the space between the front of the garden and the glads. He was curious to see the back garden, certain it was magnificent.

Mr. Green eventually opened the front door and stepped onto the porch, closing the door behind him.

"Forgive my rudeness. My wife has been quite upset. We all have. I've given her one of the tablets the doctor left. She should be asleep shortly."

"As I said, I just need a bit of information. There was

a ladder laying in Nolan's back yard. Do you know if it belonged to him?"

"One ladder looks pretty much the same as another. I know he had one. New last year. Number of the rungs on the old one were broken and rotting, so he replaced it."

Hodgins pictured the ladder as he made notes. The one in the yard wasn't very weathered, so it might be the new one.

"Don't suppose you know where he kept it?"

"I've seen him drag it out of the cellar once or twice. Now that you mention it, he did have it out the other day. Fixing some shutters before the storm. I remember looking out the window and laughing. He was still up on the ladder when the first bit of rain hit. He dang near fell off trying to hurry down. Left it up against the house."

Green blanched. "Is that how that monster got in? That's the first time I recall seeing Kendall be so careless. He must be beside himself."

Hodgins didn't answer. "Did you see anyone around the house Wednesday night?"

"No. The wife closed the drapes and I lit the lanterns. She did some knitting and I read the paper. The only sound was the rain pounding down on the roof and the wind howling. Didn't see or hear anything else. Lucky for me the storm didn't cause any damage here."

"Yes, I can see that. Only a few broken flowers." Hodgins pointed out the broken glads.

Green moved closer to the flower garden. "Oh, my poor flowers. I didn't see them. Oh well, they'll do fine in a vase for a few days."

"One last question. Did Nolan leave his daughter at home often?"

"Yes. He travelled a fair bit — salesman. She wasn't alone though. His sister stayed with her after his wife, Ruth, passed."

"Sister? First I've heard about any sister. Do you know why she didn't stay this time?"

"She died about a month or so ago."

Hodgins made a few more notes before shoving his notebook into his jacket pocket. "Thank you for your time. I'll return in a few days when your wife has recovered from the shock."

As he left, he could hear Green muttering to himself as he tended his broken gladiolas.

CHAPTER 8

Hodgins sat at his desk glancing at the clock every few minutes waiting for the Board of Trade to open. He knew from years of experience that interviewing businessmen and politicians was quite often unpleasant, unproductive, and frequently landed him in the Inspector's office. It had to be done though, unfortunately more often than he liked.

The hands of the clock finally approached nine. He'd heard Howland went to the Board office most days, so he was sure of a meeting as long as Hodgins was there when the office opened.

He walked to his office door and looked around the station house for Barnes. Several young constables were gathered together exchanging stories about the previous days arrests. They had some sort of competition going to see who had the strangest case.

"Barnes," Hodgins called. "Over here."

Barnes raced across the room, tripping over a chair along the way. "Sir?"

"How'd you like to accompany me to the Trade office to interview Howland? If we leave now we'll arrive as they're opening up."

Barnes' mouth opened and closed twice, but no words came out. He slowly shook his head.

"That wasn't a question, lad."

"Y-y-y-yes, Sir. I'll just grab my notebook."

"Don't look so scared. You were fine when you accompanied me to speak with Smythe and Flanagan last January. Both were businessmen."

"But Sir, that was just a small town. Mr. Howland is on the Board of Trade in Toronto. The president! He's much more important."

"Balderdash. He's just a man like you and me. I've heard he's quite pleasant. Nothing to be worried about. We're just going to ask him about the house, not arrest him."

The two men headed off to the Exchange Buildings at thirty-four Wellington Street East. Hodgins enjoyed the sunshine and walked briskly while whistling a snappy tune. Barnes lagged behind and frequently had to trot to catch up.

They headed down Parliament Street, taking several twists and turns down to King Street and towards St. James Cathedral.

"Magnificent building," Hodgins said to Barnes as he slowed to a stop opposite the main entrance. He pointed up at the tall tower.

"It's over three hundred feet tall you know."

"Yes, Sir. I've passed it often and spoken with the vicar several times. I know all about it. For example, did you know it's made from Ohio sandstone? Supposed to be the tallest in all Canada. Imagine that."

"Wouldn't surprise me," Hodgins replied. "Come along now. I want to speak with Howland before he gets too busy."

The Cathedral was only a few blocks from the Exchange Building on Wellington Street and they were at their destination in no time. The directory on the wall indicated Howland was on the second floor.

They went up the staircase and Hodgins admired the carving on the thick oak railing. He ran his fingers over it as he made his way up. Mr. Howland was getting ready to go to an appointment. Howland's office door was open and he'd overheard Hodgins speaking with his secretary.

"Let them in," he called out. "I can spare a few minutes."

Hodgins turned away from the secretary and walked into Howland's office. Barnes hesitated, but the glare from the pinch-nosed man sitting behind the small desk in the outer office made him scurry after the detective.

"A few questions Mr. Howland. Won't take long. I just need to know about the house you purchased on Duchess Street."

"It's an investment. A rental property. Why are the police interested in it?"

"Did you read about the young girl who was murdered earlier in the week?"

Howland shook his head and shrugged. "Too busy to read the papers lately."

"Next door to your house. Footprints in the mud indicate the person responsible may have hidden inside the house. We'd like your permission to enter and have a look around."

"Certainly. By all means. The estate agent is still trying to rent it out." He scribbled a quick note on a piece of his personalized stationery. "Here, give this to him and he'll hand over a key. His name and address are included in the note." He gave the paper to Hodgins who passed it over to Barnes.

"You know, I've never even seen the house. I hope you don't believe I was involved?" He laughed nervously. "You don't need to mention my name, do you? Wouldn't look good, you know?" As an afterthought he added, "I must give the family my condolences. Can't image what they're going through."

Hodgins thanked him for his time and they made their way back outside.

"I don't think he was involved, Sir."

"Why do you say that Barnes?"

Barnes scrunched his mouth and thought for a moment. "Well, he's a respectable business man, with a very important job." Barnes held up his hand. "I know what you're going to say. Respectable men have been known to commit crimes. It just don't feel right. Thinking of him as a murderer I mean. Nothing specific. I just believed it when he said he bought the house and was trying to rent it through an estate agent."

Hodgins nodded. "So you don't believe he ever set foot inside the vacant house?"

"No, Sir. I mean yes. I believe he never went inside. I don't think he's ever seen the house. Bought it sight-unseen. I'd like to speak with the estate agent though. His office is practically around the corner."

Hodgins put his hand on Barnes' shoulder and stopped walking. Barnes took one more step, then stopped.

"Sir?"

Hodgins smiled. "You're thinking it through. I believe Howland too, but I'd like to find out what the estate agent has to say. I'll let you take care of that while I check on a few other things. I'd like to find the lodgers that were at the boarding house that night. Also want to speak with Olivia's friends. See if they know anything. Maybe she mentioned someone she was afraid of. So far everything points to this not being random."

They walked up Church Street and parted company when they reached number twenty. Barnes went inside and Hodgins made his way back to forty-one Duchess Street to speak with Flossie again. A small sign nailed beside the door said *walk in*. He knocked and went inside.

"Hello? Miss O'Hara?"

"Just one minute."

Hodgins peeked into the room to his right. There were several chairs near the fireplace and a small table and two chairs in front of the window. A checkerboard sat on the table, the pieces set up, ready for a new game. The room was not filled with expensive furnishings, but everything looked clean and tidy. Miss O'Hara wasn't as nervous as she was when he interviewed her earlier.

She seemed to be a very please woman, and rather attractive as well. Hodgins imagined she got quite a few repeat gentlemen boarders.

"Are you looking for a room?"

Hodgins turned around.

"Oh, Detective. What can I do for you? I told you everything the other day. I'm terribly upset that I shirked my responsibility and left Miss Nolan alone. Mr. Nolan trusted me. I let him down and Olivia paid for it. I can't even dare to show my face. Everyone must think me a terrible person." She sniffled and her eyes became moist.

"Perhaps you can be of assistance and help us find her killer. I'm hoping you can fill in a few blanks for me." He pulled out his notebook and searched for the pages he filled during their earlier interview.

He stopped and tapped his finger on one of the pages in his notebook. "Here it is. You said Olivia was spending that day with friends. Do you know their names?"

"I believe she mentioned Lucy and Betsy. Lucy Armstrong and Betsy Scott. I'm afraid I don't know where they live. She mentioned another girl but I don't remember her name."

"What about the people who were staying here that night? Are they still here?"

"No. Mr. Webster left Tuesday, but Mrs. Phillips is still here. She stays whenever she visits her daughter and grand-daughter. They have a tiny one-room flat so there's no room for her. They live only a few blocks away."

"Do you have an address for Mr. Webster? Where he lives? What he does?"

"I have his address in my files. He lives somewhere in Kingston. Sells musical instruments. Please, sit down and I'll fetch it." Flossie hurried down the hall and Hodgins walked over to the table in front of the window to enjoy the breeze.

She came back carrying a tray with two glasses of lemonade. "I thought you might enjoy something cool." She placed the tray on top of the checkerboard and took a piece of paper from her pocket.

"I've written down his address for you. He comes here every other Friday and goes back home the following Tuesday."

Hodgins took the paper, copied the address in his notebook, then folded it and tucked it between the pages. He put the book on the table and picked up one of the glasses. The lemonade wasn't too sweet, but it wasn't too tart either. He hadn't realized how hot and thirsty he was until he put the empty glass on the tray.

Flossie smiled. "I'm glad you enjoyed it. Would you like another?"

Embarrassed that he guzzled it down in one go, he quickly got up.

"No, thank you. It was delicious." He picked up his notebook and headed back to the station house.

CHAPTER 9

Hodgins waited impatiently while one of the constables searched the City Directory. He drummed his fingers on his desk top and flipped through his notes without really reading them. He hoped that Olivia's friends knew something, anything, that would help locate the killer.

An hour later he had a list on his desk. There were only a handful of Scott's listed, but he had to turn the page over to see the full list of Armstrong's.

He counted – thirty four.

At least the constable had the sense to list the address and occupation of each one. He skimmed the short list first – something stood out.

The second name on the list had a familiar connection. Mr. J.G. Scott, barrister, and clerk on the Executive Council under Howland. Hodgins circled it. He wasn't sure if Olivia would have friends in such circles, considering where she lived. But did they always live there? *Another question for Nolan.*

If he didn't come back to Toronto soon, Hodgins knew he'd have to make use of the train schedule and go up to Woodbridge. He looked over the other Scotts. None lived in St. David's Ward, so he continued on to the Armstrongs.

About half way down the list he found James Armstrong, 162 Duchess St. He circled it. He had two possibilities, but he was hesitant about Mr. Scott. He decided to hold off checking on Scott and headed down to Duchess Street to find Lucy Armstrong. She would lead him to Betsy and confirm if it was the same Scott family. Hodgins hoped it wasn't the lawyer.

He glanced at the clock. Half past twelve. He decided to grab a quick bite from one of the street vendors down on Queen Street, then continue down to Duchess Street. The Armstrong's should be through with their meal by the time he arrived.

* * *

Hodgins walked across Queen while munching on a beef pie. He turned down George, then walked along Duchess looking for the Armstrong house and cursed himself when he realized he was at the wrong end. Olivia lived at number forty-one and Lucy was at one hundred sixty-two. He could have saved time if he had just stayed on Parliament. At least it gave him time to eat his pie.

He walked almost the entire length of Duchess before finding the house, a single storey clap-board just before Parliament. Hopefully Lucy was at home and not out with friends. If she was anything like his daughter, she'd be at the pond cooling off.

He knocked and waited. He could hear raised voices, then someone came clomping towards the door. He was surprised when a woman appeared. He was certain it had been a large man walking down the hall. She was quite tall and somewhat overweight. There were bags under her eyes and he could hear children's screams coming from somewhere inside. She tucked some stray hairs into the loose bun on the back of her head and shifted the baby she held against her ample hip.

"Yes?" The word dragged out, revealing how tired she must be.

He showed his badge. "Do you have a daughter named Lucy?"

"Lord, what's that girl done now?"

"She's not in any trouble. I'd like to speak to her about Olivia."

She turned her head and yelled, "Lucy, there's a copper out here what wants to talk to ya 'bout Olivia." She closed the door and went back inside, leaving Hodgins standing on the step.

He could hear muffled yelling, followed by the sound of a hand hitting flesh. A young girl opened the door. Her eyes were red and she was rubbing her cheek.

"Mama said you want to speak to me about Olivia?" she asked softly.

"Can you think of anyone who would've wanted to hurt Olivia?"

"No." Lucy sniffled and wiped her sleeve under her nose.

"Did she have a beau? Did any of the boys from school pester her?"

Lucy hesitated. "No. Nobody from school. Can I go now?" She turned and looked at the door. "Mama needs me to help."

Hodgins felt she was hiding something, but didn't want to push her. Not just yet. Clearly she was afraid. *Afraid of her mother, or someone else?* He needed to speak with her when she felt free to answer his questions.

"Just one more question, then you can go. Can you tell me where Betsy lives?"

"Somewhere on Shuter Street. Never bin there. Gotta go."

Lucy turned and ran back inside. He could hear more shouting as he walked away. Hodgins removed the folded list from his notebook and searched through the long list of Scotts, looking for an address on Shuter. He stumbled as he walked off the curb at Berkeley.

"Blast. John G. Scott. The man on Howland's council. And a barrister."

Hodgins didn't want to get on the wrong side of a barrister. At least he wouldn't likely be home this early. He turned on Sherbourne and walked up to Shuter, looking for number eighty-one as he made his way west.

He wondered how someone in Lucy's situation could have met and become friends with the daughter of a barrister. They lived in different wards and wouldn't have attended the same schools or social events. He doubted Lucy had ever attended a social event.

Hodgins watched the numbers decrease and saw eighty-seven as he approached Jarvis. *Not much farther.* Unlike Duchess Street, most of the homes along this section of Shuter were brick. *Definitely a higher class neighbourhood.*

He stopped in front of a yellow brick two-storey house. The house seemed rather plain. The front was completely flat. No porch or even a crown over the doorway. It's only feature was the tiny peak and window at the roofline. The house beside it on the corner was much grander. The extra floor on top gave it a finished look.

He glanced down the street and noticed the tall tower

of St. Michael's Cathedral. *All in all a very nice neighbourhood.*

Not wanting to risk being there when Mr. Scott arrived, Hodgins stopped putting off the visit to the lawyer's home and walked up to the door. His knock was answered by a middle-aged housekeeper.

Hodgins always kept a few cards in his pocket for just this sort of occasion and handed one to the housekeeper as an introduction. "I'd like to speak with Miss Betsy Scott."

She read the card and looked Hodgins up and down. Hodgins figured she was deciding whether or not to admit him.

"Wait here please."

Hodgins stepped inside before she could close the door in his face. She gave him a dirty look then slowly walked down the hall and into a room off to the right. It was much nicer inside.

The floor was polished to a shine, and the vase sitting on the side table looked quite expensive. There was a doorway on the other side of the table. He took a few steps in so he could get a look inside.

The fireplace looked like it might be marble. A large portrait of a man hung over the mantle. He suspected it was Mr. Scott as the gentleman was holding a law book. He heard the rustling of skirts and turned his attention down the hall. A very elegant, but stern looking woman approached. She stood straight and tall, yet seemed to float. Her shoes made no sound on the bare wooden floor. He guessed the jewels around her neck were genuine emeralds.

"I understand you wish to speak with my daughter. She's only a child. What could you want with her?"

Hodgins quickly removed his hat. "I'm investigating the death of her friend, Olivia Nolan. Is she home? It's very important."

Her face softened. "Olivia. Tragic. Betsy is too upset to see anyone."

"It's crucial that I speak with her as soon as possible. Every day wasted puts us farther away from finding the man who did it."

Mrs. Scott paused to consider the request. "Very well, but I insist I stay with her."

"Yes, of course. Thank you."

Mrs. Scott gestured to the room Hodgins had been looking at. "Wait in here."

Hodgins stepped in to wait for her to return with Betsy. He was immediately drawn to the large bookcase that practically covered the south wall. The shelves were filled with law books. He ran his fingers over the spines, remembering his year at Osgood Hall. If circumstances had been different, he might be living in a house like this. He heard voices in the hall and moved away from the books.

Mrs. Scott returned with her daughter. Betsy was very much like her mother. The same chestnut hair, perfect posture and skin like porcelain. No doubt there would be a long line of suitors soon.

Mrs. Scott and Betsy sat on the sofa. Betsy reached over and took her mother's hand for support.

"Please be seated," Mrs. Scott said.

"Hello Miss Scott. My name is Detective Hodgins. I'm trying to find out who harmed your friend. Would you mind answering a few questions?"

Betsy looked at her mother. Mrs. Scott nodded.

"How long have you been friends with Miss Nolan?"

"Only since last summer. Mother was shopping for fabric and I went with her. It was hot so I went up the street to the druggist. They have a soda fountain. Olivia was in there with her father. He was speaking with the chemist so we chatted while we were waiting. We've been friends ever since."

So that explains how the girls met. Happenstance, nothing more. Hodgins remembered how Lucy faltered when he asked her about boys bothering Olivia and decided to try a different tactic.

"Lucy told me about the boy that was bothering Olivia."

Betsy gasped. "She did? But he wasn't a boy, exactly."

Interesting.

"Lucy couldn't remember his name. Do you? Did you ever meet him?"

"Olivia called him Johnny. I only saw him once. He was quite handsome. He kept asking Olivia to marry him, but she wasn't interested."

"What did you mean when you said he wasn't exactly a boy? How old is he?"

Betsy bit her bottom lip while she thought about it. "Well, he was older, maybe twenty." Her eyes grew wide. "Do you think he did it? He's seen me with Olivia. Do you think he'll come after me?" Betsy started to cry.

"I'm sure you have nothing to worry about." Seeing how distressed she had become, he decided to end the interview before Mrs. Scott did. He stood up.

"I won't keep you any longer. Thank you for your time. I'll see myself out."

CHAPTER 10

Barnes was waiting when Hodgins arrived back at the station. He hurried over to update Hodgins about the estate agent.

"Quite a chatty fellow is Mr. Lake. Almost talked me into renting a house. Anyway, he confirmed that Mr. Howland purchased the house on his recommendation. Finally had someone interested in renting it, until the murder."

Barnes stood at Hodgins' desk waiting for him to say something. Hodgins nodded but didn't respond to his report. Instead, he grumbled something about Mr. Nolan leaving town last Saturday. Three days had passed and he still had not returned.

"I just don't understand it," Hodgins said. "How can the man just up and leave when his daughter's been murdered? I know I'd constantly be asking questions, wondering what the police were doing, and when I could bury her. I don't think he's made any arrangements. When would he have had the time?"

Hodgins slammed his fist on the desk.

"What is wrong with that man? I need to talk to him *now*." He scribbled on a piece of paper and thrust it at Barnes.

"Send this telegram at once. He said he can be contacted through the Post Office in Woodbridge. If he doesn't reply by the end of the day, I'm taking a trip up there myself. In the meanwhile I guess I'll try to track down John Webster."

Barnes read the note before leaving, just in case he couldn't read the hurried writing. Satisfied, he hurried off to the telegraph office.

Frustration gnawed at Hodgins. Needing to do something other than grumble, he went home to pack a bag then headed to the train station for the next train to Kingston to look for Webster.

He arrived late in the evening. After chatting with a railway employee to get directions to a hotel and the police station, Hodgins got a carriage at the Grand Trunk station and headed down Montreal Street into the heart of Kingston. He went straight to the Grand Hotel, glad that the expense would be covered. For the first time in a quite a while, he slept in.

Between working the murder case and moving into a new home, he was worn out. Hodgins was surprised to see it was after eight when he woke up. Normally the aromas coming from the kitchen were enough to rouse him, no matter how tired. Unfortunately he couldn't smell Cordelia's cooking from Kingston.

After a leisurely breakfast, he walked to the police station, hoping they would be willing to help with his inquiries. He filled them in and said he was trying to find a person of interest. Someone who had been staying across the street from the scene of the crime at the time.

They were more than happy to oblige, and with the assistance of one of their constables, Hodgins had a list of establishments handling musical instruments. Fortunately it was not long; two dealers and three manufacturers. He started with the dealers – they weren't very far.

G. Adams was at the top of the list, so he headed there. Hodgins thought it funny that Adams also dealt in sewing machines and agricultural implements. *How the devil do they connect?*

The conversation with Adams was short. Yes, John Webster had worked there, but he fired him about a year earlier.

"Do you have any daughters Detective?"

"Yes. Sara. She just turned nine."

"Few more years and you'll understand better. Just wait 'till the lads start hanging around." Adams tugged at his shirt collar and lowered his voice. "Had a spot of trouble two years ago. My girl's got a wild streak. Some blighter seduced her." His hands balled into fists and he started to bang them against the arms of the chair. "Had to send her away for a bit. Couldn't have that happen again."

He wouldn't go into further detail. Adams told him Webster was currently employed with James Purdy, right across the road.

Before he made his way to Purdy's he thought about what Betsy had told him. Someone named Johnny had been bothering Olivia. *Could John Webster be that Johnny?* Hodgins pulled out his pocket watch to check the time. Eleven thirty. He'd speak with Purdy, then find something to eat.

As this was his first visit to Kingston, his thoughts wandered, thinking about everything that had happened over here in recent years. Uppermost in his mind were the Prime Ministers. John MacDonald, Canada's first appointed Prime Minister was from Kingston, as was the current Prime Minister, Alexander McKenzie. *Seems the Scots are taking over the country.*

He found Purdy's establishment easily but had to wait before he could speak with the owner. Hodgins enjoyed the company of a rather attractive young woman who was trying to concentrate on some paperwork.

The door to the inner office finally opened and two men came out. They shook hands and the younger one left, waving to the young woman and ignoring Hodgins. The elder one turned to Hodgins.

"I'm James Purdy. What can I help you with? Sewing machines? Musical instruments? How about some modern farming equipment? We sell only the highest quality."

Hodgins showed his badge. "I need to speak to you about one of your salesmen. John Webster."

Purdy rolled his eyes. "Come into my office and tell me what he's been up to this time."

Purdy sat in a rather plush looking, broken-in brown leather chair behind a large oak desk. Hodgins sat in a rigid wooden one opposite him.

"What's this all about then?"

"I'm only making inquires. A young girl was murdered last week and Webster was staying in a boarding house just up the street. He might have seen or heard something that could help with my investigation. I have reason to believe he was acquainted with her. He stayed at the boarding house on a regular basis. Is he about?"

Purdy steepled his hands and tapped his fingertips.

"Young girl you say?"

"Yes. Fifteen or sixteen."

"Hmm, mighty young for Webster," Purdy said. "I'm

afraid he's on the road. I like to keep him travelling."

"Good salesman?"

"Better than most. The only reason I keep him really."

Hodgins detected something in Purdy's face. Something he wasn't saying.

"I understand from Abrams he had a spot of trouble with Webster and let him go. Are you having the same bother?"

"Did you see that young lady in the outer office?"

Hodgins smiled. "Hard to miss. Very attractive."

"My daughter. I keep Webster on the road to minimize any contact he might have with her, if you get my meaning."

"If he's only a fair salesman, why not just let him go?"

"As I said, he's not great, but he's actually my top seller. Relies a lot on his looks and charm. He should be spending more time selling the product, not himself. He definitely has a way with the ladies. Doesn't matter the age. A lot of the music teachers are women and he's managed to sell some of my more expensive instruments to places we've previously never been able to get orders from."

Hodgins laughed. "So you're taking advantage of *him* before he takes advantage of your daughter."

Purdy tapped the side of his nose and winked. "Spot on. Might even get him selling the sewing machines to the seamstresses. Don't think he'd be any good selling my farm implements though." Purdy started laughing. "He'd probably get run through with a pitch fork."

Hodgins was getting more and more curious to meet this Webster character. "When do you expect him back? Can I have his address?"

"Won't be back for a few days yet. When he's in town, he stays with his folks. They live on Pine Street." Purdy gave Hodgins directions.

"You married Detective?"

The question caught him off guard. "Yes, he said slowly. "Why do you ask?"

"Got a lovely sewing machine just in. Latest model." Purdy wrote on the back of a business card and held it out towards Hodgins. "Give this to one of the dealers I've listed in Toronto and you'll get a good discount."

Hodgins smiled and took the card. "Have to check with my wife."

They shook hands and Hodgins went in search of a meal. The Grand Hotel had good food so he decided to eat there. Easier to submit one bill for the hotel and his meals when he got back.

As he walked, he read the card before putting it in his pocket. Cordelia just might like her own sewing machine so she didn't have to keep going to her mother's.

After his slightly pricey meal at the hotel Hodgins walked down to Routley's and bought a doll for Sara and some earrings for Cordelia. He knew he shouldn't be spending his money on items they didn't need, but he couldn't resist.

Hodgins went back to the hotel and collected his satchel before hailing a passing hansom cab to go see Webster's parents. When he arrived, he asked the driver to wait as he wouldn't be long.

He left his card and asked them to have their son get in touch as soon as he was back in Toronto next week. Hodgins climbed back into the buggy and told the driver to take him to the Grand Trunk Railway Station. He wanted to catch the evening train so he could be back in Toronto by morning.

CHAPTER 11

Hodgins arrived home in the wee hours Wednesday morning and had only managed a few house sleep on the train. He didn't want to disturb Cordelia, so he didn't bother going to bed. He made himself as comfortable as possible in the drawing room and tried to catch a bit more sleep before she woke.

He was up before Cordelia so he made his own breakfast. Lingering in the kitchen, he waited for his wife and daughter to rise. He was in no rush to get to the station and poured himself a second cup of tea.

Cordelia came down an hour later. She could tell he had something he wanted to talk about, but Hodgins refused to speak until Sara was at the table. He was smiling, so she knew it wasn't anything bad, and he had a small, oddly shaped package sitting on the table in front of him.

"Can you give me a little hint?" she asked.

"No, wait for Sara." He leaned back in the chair, crossed his arms over his chest, and smiled.

Cordelia went upstairs to hurry Sara along.

Sara skipped into the kitchen ahead of her mother and kissed her father before sitting at the table.

"Good morning, Daddy." She eyed the package. "Is that for me?"

Cordelia stood behind Sara, waiting to find out what was going on. Hodgins slowly loosened the knot in the string. Sara squirmed in her chair.

"What is it Daddy?

Hodgins slid the package over to Sara. She pulled the paper back and squealed in delight. Sara got off the chair and threw her arms around him.

"Thank you Daddy. She's beautiful." She sat back down, picked up the doll, and wrapped its long blond curls around her fingers.

"Bertie, you spoil that child sometimes. With this new house we can't afford to be so frivolous."

Since Cordelia seemed so concerned about their finances, he figured it was time to fill her in. Hodgins had never told her just how much money he had been able to save while they stayed at her parents all those years. They had no mortgage to worry about and there was still a fair bit of money in the bank. It wouldn't last forever, but they could occasionally afford a few indulgences. He decided they'd discuss their finances once he solved Olivia's murder and he could give Delia all his attention.

He reached into the inside pocket of his jacket and pulled out a small box.

"Then I suppose I should return this?"

He handed it to Cordelia. She took the lid off and gasped.

"Really, you shouldn't have bought them."

Cordelia held up the earrings. Two thin silver chains about one inch long, with a pearl dangling on each end. "They are quite breathtaking though."

She kissed him, then showed them to Sara. She held them up against the doll's head and they both giggled.

"What will you be busying yourself with today?" he asked.

Cordelia sighed. "Over to Mother's again. I need to finish sewing the draperies. I'll be glad once everything is finally finished."

Hodgins smiled as he thought about the card Mr. Purdy had given him. He was certain Delia was forgive him one final surprise. "I'm sure it will get easier soon."

Cordelia put the earrings back in their box and moved Sara's doll off the table. Once breakfast was over, He reluctantly headed to the station house.

* * *

Hodgins went directly to Barnes' desk to inquire about

Nolan.

"Have you received a reply to the telegram yet?"

"Yes, Sir. Said he won't be back for several more days."

"Blast that man. What's wrong with him? He doesn't seem to care that someone murdered his daughter. How can he be so callous?"

Hodgins banged his fist on the desk.

"I need to speak with him *now*. Do we even know who he works for? What he sells? All I know is he's a salesman. Travels a lot."

Barnes flipped through his notebook. "According to neighbours he sells one of those patent medicines. An elixir if you will."

Hodgins groaned. "Don't tell me he's one of those charlatans selling cure-alls that cure nothing?"

"Not at all. I haven't had time to confirm it, but one of his neighbours mentioned he works for Lyman's. Very respectable firm. Office in the St. Lawrence Building over on Front."

"Lyman's you say? I think I'll stroll over and see what they can tell me about him. While I'm gone, why don't you go down to the vacant house beside Nolan's and see if you can find anything inside that could help with the case."

* * *

Hodgins entered the office of Lyman Brothers & Co., introduced himself to the elderly clerk, and asked to speak with one of the owners. The clerk explained that the owners were in the main office in Quebec, but one of the sons was available.

The clerk rose from his chair and hobbled over to the inner office. He knocked and entered. Hodgins could hear murmuring through the closed door. A few moments later the clerk came out.

"Mr. Lyman will see you now."

Hodgins smiled at the clerk and went into the office.

"Detective Hodgins, what can I do for you? I'm Henry Lyman. I assume it has something to do with the murder of Nolan's daughter? Terrible tragedy. I know my father and uncle would like to attend the funeral. Do you know when it will be?"

Hodgins shrugged his shoulders. "Unfortunately she's still with the coroner. Nolan left town and there's no one else to release the body to. He should be back soon. What can you tell me about Kendall Nolan? What kind of man is he?"

"I'm afraid I don't know him personally. I work at the Montreal office. Only in Toronto a short while. Making the rounds, checking in to make sure everything is running smoothly. I'll be going up to Ottawa tomorrow, then back home."

"I see. Is there someone here I could talk to that knows him? I understand he travels quite a bit. Does he have a set route? Regular customers he visits?"

"My clerk should be able to help you there. He's been here since the company started and knows everyone. I do know Nolan is our best salesman in the region. Number three overall. His name comes up quite often."

Lyman got up and went to the office door to speak to his clerk. "The detective has some questions about Nolan. Please assist him all you can." He turned back to Hodgins.

"I have several reports to write before the end of the day. I'll leave you in the capable hands of Mr. Fuller."

Hodgins knew a dismissal when he heard one. He thanked Mr. Lyman and went back to the outer office.

"Do you know Mr. Nolan's customers and routes?"

"Yes, Sir." Fuller rummaged through a cabinet drawer and pulled out a file. He brought it back to his desk and spread out the papers.

"Our experienced salesmen don't have any set route or schedule. They just go by past orders and know when to pay a visit to their customers. The new ones start out on a set schedule, but once they know their customers, they figure out what route and times work best. Nolan is quite experienced and has had the same stops for several years."

Hodgins looked over the reports. Nolan had quite a large territory to cover. No wonder he was away from home so much.

"Might I trouble you for a copy of his customers, addresses and how often they place orders?"

"Certainly."

While the clerk wrote out the list, Hodgins asked him about Nolan.

"What can you tell me about Kendall Nolan? Is he a hard worker? Sociable?"

"He comes in fairly often to get more supplies. Works really hard to stay on top. Pleasant chap. Speaks of his daughter often." Fuller stopped writing and looked up at Hodgins.

"Can't imagine what he's going through. He was quite distressed when Mrs. Nolan passed. Then his sister, now his daughter. She came in with him a few times. Very polite and pretty. Such a shame."

He finished writing the list and handed it to Hodgins. "Is there anything else?"

"No, not at the moment. If I need anything I'll send one of the constables over."

"Do you know who did it?"

"Still making inquiries. Thank you for your time."

Hodgins was still annoyed that Nolan was staying in

Woodbridge for so long. As he left Lyman Brothers & Co. he grumbled and mumbled to himself. Hodgins found it impossible to get inside Nolan's head. He hadn't realized how loudly he was grumbling until he passed a lady who reprimanded him for his foul language.

He needed to find that man and soon. Remembering the schedule he recalled seeing a late morning train and hurried to Union Station. A train was leaving in thirty minutes.

While waiting for the train to pull in he read over the list Fuller had given him, looking for clients around Woodbridge. He found two: a druggist, S.J. Snell, and a Dr. J. Wilkinson.

Hodgins sat on a nearby bench and opened his notebook to add to his notes. Observations and Questions. Not many observation, but a lot of questions.

The more he thought about how Nolan was acting, the angrier he got. Slamming his notebook closed he jammed it in his jacket pocket. He heard a small rip and swore. Hodgins took a deep breath and held it for a few seconds, then slowly let it out. He felt a little better. A few more deep breaths and he felt more like himself. Examining his pocket revealed only minor damage. *Just a few broken threads.* He wondered if he could repair it himself so Cordelia didn't find out. She had enough to do without having extra sewing on account of his temper.

He walked over to the schedule board and noted the time of the last train back. He hoped he could make it as it would be very expensive to hire a buggy to return home. He had to be careful with his spending and he wasn't certain a long buggy ride was an expense he would be reimbursed for.

The thirty minute wait went fairly fast and Hodgins was soon on his way to Woodbridge. He checked his pocket watch. It would take about an hour to get there. That didn't leave him much time to find Nolan.

As soon as he arrived he inquired as to the location of the post office and was happy to discover it was not far from the station. Hopefully someone there knew exactly where Nolan could be located.

It was a scorching, hot, sunny day, and unfortunately there were no clouds. The shade from the trees and buildings along Pine Street did nothing to help combat the heat of summer.

When he arrived at the post office he found the door propped open and a number of people inside. The ladies fanned themselves and the clerk wiped his brow continually. He never seemed to get every drop of sweat.

Hodgins waited his turn impatiently, tapping his foot and looking at the cuckoo clock on the wall behind the counter every few minutes. When he was finally served, his frustration grew. He showed the clerk his badge.

"Do you know Mr. Kendall Nolan?"

"Yes, I know Mr. Nolan. Not well mind you. Comes in every week or two to pick up mail."

Hodgins made a note in his trusty notebook. "Every week or two you say? What about his address? Where does he live?"

The clerk shrugged. "Sorry. Don't know. He wasn't one for passing the time of day, ya know? Just picked up his mail and left."

Hodgins slapped his notebook on the counter. "Blast and damnation!"

"Such language. Should be ashamed of yourself."

Hodgins turned and discovered a lady standing behind him. He guessed she was in her sixties at the very least.

"I'm terribly sorry. Please excuse me." Hodgins turned red from both the heat and his embarrassment. He turned back to the counter and picked up his book.

"I wish these small towns had some sort of law enforcement. Make my job that much easier." He nodded at the clerk and avoided looking at the lady waiting her turn as he hurried out of the post office and off to his next stop.

Neither the druggist nor the doctor had seen Nolan

for weeks. Didn't expect him until next month, and neither knew where he lived. The only good thing for Hodgins was he wouldn't have to worry about missing the train home.

He trudged back along Pine and veered off towards the tavern. He noticed there seemed to be a tavern near every train station. He figured if he had to wait for the train, he may as well have a beer or two to help him cool down. Something gnawed at the back of his mind and he couldn't quite put his finger on it.

Rather than dwell on it, he took out the list of customers and tried to figure out where Nolan might have gone. He read over the dates. Most of the customers placed large enough orders that Nolan didn't have to visit any one of them too frequently.

Something twigged.

He looked at the order dates for Snell and Wilkinson. Nolan only came to Woodbridge every six or seven weeks yet the clerk at the post office said he picked up mail every week or two. *Why would Nolan pick up mail here frequently? He doesn't even live here.*

CHAPTER 12

When Hodgins arrived back in Toronto, he made a quick stop at the station to see if Barnes had any news. It appeared that he too was getting frustrated.

"So many leads that all seem to go nowhere," Barnes said. "I checked both the front and back door on the vacant house. No sign of anyone breaking in. The locks weren't forced and all the windows are boarded up. Few loose boards, but none missing.

"Since the estate agent provided the key, I figured I may as well go in. Went upstairs and checked those windows. Nothing out of place. There's a thin layer of dust everywhere. No footprints. No hand marks. Doesn't appear as any furniture was moved or disturbed in any way."

Barnes flipped the page of his notebook and kept talking.

"I circled around the outside again and it does appear as though someone else had done so, probably looking for an easy way in. More prints the same size as the ones we saw earlier."

He turned his book to show Hodgins his sketch.

"See here?" Barnes pointed to an 'x'. "I made a mark where there were prints around the windows. There, and here too."

"What about the laneway?"

"Still full of mud."

Hodgins nodded. "Good work. At least we were right to think someone wanted to hide in the empty house."

Since nothing new had turned up, Hodgins decided to head home after one final stop. He took the card from Purdy out of his pocket and read the back. Mr. Purdy had written the name and address of two places in Toronto that sold his sewing machines.

Even though he knew they still had money in the bank, he would have to watch is spending. A sewing machine was something his wife would use for years, so it was worth the small extravagance.

He went to the closest shop and showed the card. The clerk fetched the owner and Hodgins was treated like upper-class. He didn't bother to tell them he was just a copper.

The store had received a delivery that morning, and the shipment contained two of the new models. Hodgins gave the owner his address and arranged for delivery

Saturday. It was his day off and he wanted to be there when it arrived.

* * *

When he opened his front door, the house was unusually quiet. No aromas drifted down from the kitchen, even though he could hear faint sounds as Cordelia prepared their evening meal. Only the dog had taken the time to greet him at the door, and that was with less gusto than usual. Seemed the heat was affecting everyone.

When he walked into the kitchen he saw Sara sitting at the table peeling and cutting carrots. Cordelia turned to greet him. She brushed some loose strands of hair from her face with the back of her hand. Several stuck in place.

"Oh dear. I can tell by the look on your face you've had a bad day."

A weak 'harrumph' was all Hodgins could manage as he sat down. His usual walk from the trolley had not cleared his mind this time.

"I made lemonade Daddy. I'll pour you some."

Sara hopped off the chair and walked to the ice box, plucking a glass from the cupboard shelf along the way. The ice box wasn't very big, but it was quite handy. Something his mother-in-law didn't even have. It had a compartment on the top for the ice and a spigot so you could pour out the cold water as it melted. The double doors on the front opened to reveal two shelves. A glass pitcher sat on the top shelf.

Sara poured out the lemonade and took it to her father. He downed it in one go. *Not quite as good as Miss O'Hara's.* He had sense enough not to say that out loud.

"Thank you Sara. It was just what I needed."

Scraps had stretched out on the floor near the ice box, tongue hanging out. Hodgins got up and filled the dog's water bowl with some of the melted ice water. Scraps drank it down, then licked Hodgins' hand before stretching out across the floor.

During dinner there was little conversation. Sara chatted a bit about her new doll. One of her friends had come over and they played with it in the morning, then Cordelia took them down to the beach in the afternoon.

"How are the draperies coming along?" Hodgins asked. He wanted to tell Cordelia about his latest purchase but decided to keep it a surprise.

"Slow. I just couldn't bear the thought of being enveloped in all that cloth on such a hot day. And you know how mother's Irish temper flares up in this heat. Best to stay away. Hopefully it cools down soon. I would like to get them finished. They'll help keep the house cool."

Cordelia didn't inquire about his current case as they

both had decided not to talk about it in front of Sara. She was used to hearing them talk about the various thefts and even some murders, but this was different. They felt it best not to discuss the murder of a child when she was around. After Sara went to bed, Cordelia sat down in the drawing room to talk with her husband.

"What is bothering you so? Is it because a young girl was killed?"

"No. Well yes, but that's not all. It's her father. I just don't understand him. He asked no questions. Hasn't yelled because we haven't arrested anyone. Hasn't even asked about burying her. McKenzie wants to release her body, but Nolan has disappeared."

He paced around the room, unfastening the top two buttons on his shirt and loosening his collar. "I just can't fathom what's going through his head. He said I could contact him through the Woodbridge post office, but they have no idea where he lives. No one I spoke to does either. Even more puzzling, the post office clerk said Nolan picks up mail regularly, but his order schedule has him going up only every two months."

"That *is* puzzling. But why is he having correspondence sent there instead of his home?"

"Exactly. That's what I want, no *need*, to find out."

"I've been reading another of those delicious crime

books. The gentleman was having certain correspondence sent to his office instead of home."

"Understandable Delia. He wouldn't have business matters sent to his house. But Nolan's house is his office in a manner of speaking. Course he could have business letters sent to Lyman's."

She waved her hand, dismissing his comment. "No, you don't understand. Those letters were personal. Something he was keeping from his wife. I can't wait to find out what. Maybe Nolan has a secret. Would you mind sitting down? You're making me dizzy."

Hodgins smiled and stopped pacing. "Interesting. But why all the way up in Woodbridge? Why not right here in Toronto?"

Cordelia shrugged and smiled. "That's why you're the detective Bertie, not me."

He walked over to where she was sitting and kissed the top of her head. "Sometimes I'm glad you don't read those silly romance stories like normal women. After I check in at the station tomorrow I'll go back up and ask more questions. If he spends so much time there someone has to know something.

CHAPTER 13

Hodgins rose early and made his way to the station house. The heat had broken over night, so he walked over rather than wait for a trolley. The air was still, absent of a breeze, but the lower temperature was relief enough. Even the song of the robins seemed cheerier.

Not many people were about yet. The news boys had picked up their papers and were heading to their spots. Hodgins hailed one down, bought a paper, and tucked it under his arm.

The station house was unusually quiet. Hodgins went into the back room, made a cup of tea then went to his office. The copy of the train schedule he had picked up earlier was still laying open on his desk. He circled the time the first train headed north then checked his pocket watch. *Plenty of time yet.*

He drank his tea then went over to the maps that were piled on a table against the wall. He rummaged through them until he found one with Woodbridge on it. He figured if Nolan went to the post office often but no one knew where he lived, he must be staying out of town somewhere. *But where?*

He located a couple of possibilities. Just a little south of Woodbridge was the town of Brownsville, and another just north-east called Pine Grove. *If Nolan has a secret, is it possible he stays in one of those towns and uses the post office in Woodbridge to hide his whereabouts?*

He went back to his desk to wait for Barnes. While any of the constables would do, he preferred to use whoever was first on the scene. He seemed to be working with Barnes quite often, and that suited him fine.

The change of shift started and the door constantly opened as some of the men left and others arrived. The chattering got louder and louder. Hodgins looked up every time he heard the door. Ten minutes later Barnes arrived.

"Barnes." Hodgins waved him over. "Have you run a check on Nolan?"

Barnes came over and stood in the doorway, looking surprised. "No. I didn't think it necessary. You don't think he killed his own daughter, do you?"

"No, no. Nothing like that. But he's hiding something and I need to find out what. Use some of the boys. Check records here, and everywhere in a hundred mile radius if necessary. Pay particular attention to the Woodbridge area."

"That will take some time, Sir."

"Well you'd better get cracking then. I'm heading up there now to try and track him down. There has to be at least one person who knows where he's at." Hodgins stood and slipped the newspaper back under his arm.

"Right away, Sir." As Barnes stepped back out of Hodgins' office his heel hit the leg of a chair that had been pushed away from the desk right outside. He fell backwards, fortunately landing on the seat of the chair. Barnes turned a deep shade of red as the laugher made its way through the station.

Hodgins picked up the train schedule and slipped it in the inside pocket of his jacket. "I'm counting on you Barnes. I'm confident you'll find something right quick."

Hodgins spoke loud enough for everyone to hear, hoping it would ease some of the ribbing. He managed to hold in his laughter until he was well away.

The train ride went by fast as Hodgins became engrossed in the paper. Two young ladies out Woodford way had gone missing. Hodgins hoped they hadn't met the same fate as Olivia and would soon be found, safe and sound.

He flipped though the paper and turned to the sports. The baseball club from Brooklyn had visited Guelph and they somehow managed to beat the Guelph Maple Leafs by a whopping 15-1. He figured the Guelph team was simply worn out from winning the world championship last month in Waterdown, New York. Hodgins was just reading about the small pox breakout in Peterborough when the trained slowed for the station.

On his arrival in Woodbridge there were a surprising number of people in town. Probably trying to catch up on errands left undone due to the recent bad weather. Most were farmers or their wives.

He asked everyone if they knew Nolan and where he could find him. Person after person told him the same thing, either they didn't know him, or if they did, had no idea where he lived. For a man who was in town regularly, he didn't seem to have made any friends.

The morning dragged on until he finally had a bit of luck. One person gave him some hope. He didn't know where Nolan lived, but he had seen him in Pine Grove about a week ago, loading supplies onto a wagon.

Hodgins thanked him, then went to the livery stable to hire a buggy so he could get to the little village to the north-east. The town was larger than he expected. His first stop was the general store where Nolan had been spotted. He hoped Nolan was staying nearby.

The store had a generous wooden porch with a pair of rockers to the left of the door. A bicycle leaned against the wall off to the right. He could picture a couple of old men in the rockers passing the day, reminiscing.

He tied the horse to the post out front and went in. Only three ladies were inside. One was at the counter selling her fresh eggs to the owner. Two others were at the far side, bickering over a bolt of fabric.

Hodgins eyed the jars of candies and thought of Sara. She loved licorice and hard candies and the store had ample supply of both. He knew Cordelia would object and he really didn't want to carry it around so he continued walking around. He didn't do much shopping and was amazed at the multitude of canned goods, flour, grains, and fabric. It seemed everything a person could want was available in one spot.

As he passed the hanging weigh scale he gave it a quick poke. He looked around and was relieved to see no one had noticed his child-like behaviour. He made his way back to the front to wait for the ladies to finish their business and leave.

"Find what yer looking fer?"

"Actually, I came in search of information." Hodgins introduced himself, then continued. "Are you acquainted with Kendall Nolan? I'm told he was here recently."

"Oh my. Is something wrong? Is he in trouble? Seemed like such a nice chap."

DEATH ON DUCHESS STREET

"No, he's not in any trouble." *At least not yet.* "I'm trying to locate him. Do you know where I can find him?"

"Why yes. He has a small farm just outside town." He pointed towards the east. "Third one up the road."

Hodgins thanked the man and turned to leave.

"Won't find him here though."

Hodgins groaned. Did Nolan ever stay put? He turned back to face the grocer.

"Saw him head out 'bout an hour ago."

Hodgins wondered how a salesman could afford both a house in the city and a farm. Even a top-notch salesman wouldn't be that well off.

"Him and his wife moved in three, maybe four, years ago. She don't come in much. Nice enough looking woman."

Hodgins nodded and left. He untied the horse and got in the buggy. Frustrated, he went back to Woodbridge and sat in the tavern until the next train back to Toronto.

He re-read his notes and added a few more. Maybe Nolan's late wife had money. He'd have to see what Barnes had uncovered. *Strange. The store owner hadn't mentioned Nolan's daughter.* Maybe he didn't know she was dead. Nolan probably didn't want to talk about it.

CHAPTER 14

Hodgins arrived back at the station tired, dusty, and without any answers. He dragged himself up the steps of the building. Several desks around Barnes were covered in books and newspapers. It looked like Barnes had recruited three of the constables to help him compile a background on Nolan. Hodgins went over to see what they had found out.

"Not a lot yet, Sir," Barnes said. "We did find the church record for his marriage. Also found a little write-up in the paper." Barnes picked up a newspaper from 1858. "They had a small service at her parents home – Mr. & Mrs. Fred Johnson. Fred worked in one of the mills. Doesn't appear to have bin anythin' fancy."

"So, they weren't particularly well off then?"

"I wouldn't think so."

"Puzzling. It seems our Mr. Nolan has a farm up Woodbridge way. Town called Pine Grove." Hodgins took the paper from Barnes and read the small write-up.

"He was only a salesman. I thought maybe her family

had money."

"That is puzzling," Barnes said.

"Well, keep digging. Concentrate farther north. See what you can find."

Hodgins walked to his desk and dropped his notebook on top. He opened the drawer and took out a pad of long paper and started copying some of the notes from his book, then pinned them up on his office wall.

Somewhere between Monday evening and Tuesday morning someone climbed through Olivia's bedroom window, chased her downstairs, then killed her.

The girl wasn't interfered with, and nothing seems to have been taken from the house. Just furniture and what-not toppled over or broken. The man may have come in through the laneway.

The laneway!

He hadn't gone back to check it again. Figuring it should finally be dry enough, Hodgins left the newspaper on his desk, picked up his notebook, then hurried off to the lane.

Since there had been no rain for several days and the temperature remained high, the river of mud in the lane had practically dried up. It was hopeless to try and find footprints. They would have been washed away long since.

He examined the boards where they had been broken

off and allowed access to the back yard. He couldn't believe he missed doing that earlier. The murder of Olivia must have affected him more than he wanted to admit.

He had seen quite a number of dead children over the years, but this was the first time he had to deal with the murder of one. And it was such a brutal death. He needed to focus on his job. Try to forget the image of the young girl, all battered and bloody. Try to simply investigate. It wasn't going to be easy to put his personal feelings aside, but he had to.

Hodgins found a tiny scrap of fabric caught on the rough edges of one of the boards. It felt like flannel. Based on the height he found it snagged, it must be from someone's shirt. It wasn't much to go on and it could have been there for days, weeks even. Flannel shirts were quite common, owned by most labourers. Rather a warm fabric to be wearing in July though. Most men wore cotton.

This had to be one of the most frustrating cases he had worked on. There were next to no clues. The board cracked as he slammed his fist against it. A few flakes of whitewash floated to the ground.

"Blast and damnation." He shook his hand, then wiggled his fingers. Nothing broken, but his knuckles would be bruised for days.

So far he had only one good suspect. John Webster.

He had been giving Olivia unwanted attention and was just across the road the night she was killed. Hopefully he could track him down next week when he was back at Miss O'Hara's.

Hodgins took one last look around the outside of Nolan's house, then started back to the station. He walked east on Duchess and glanced south as he crossed Sherbourne. He could see Duke Street and remembered the painter. He had forgotten there was a man murdered nearby and they still hadn't found the person responsible. It wasn't his case, but maybe they were connected. *Carter's in charge of that one.* He decided to talk to him when he got back. See if he had any leads.

It was late in the afternoon by the time Hodgins arrived back at Station House Four. He had stopped on Queen to buy a pie from one of the street vendors and was finishing it when he entered the station. Carter was just getting ready to leave.

"Hold up a minute Carter. I'm working on a murder that might be connected to your case. That dead man from Duke Street. Mind if I look through your files?"

"That young girl? Terrible thing. Wouldn't want that one. If there's any chance you can find a connection, be my guest. Even if they ain't connected, you may notice something I've overlooked. Maybe a fresh set of eyes will help. If they are linked, we can close both in one go."

Hodgins thought about that missing woman who lived on George Street. She still hasn't been located. Could all three be connected? Hodgins wondered if it was simply a coincidence that so many things had happened in such a small radius. He hoped there wasn't a maniac running around the city.

Hodgins went to the cabinet and found the file on the painter. He took it over to his desk and laid the papers out.

McKenzie's autopsy report indicated the body had likely been in the house for a few days before he was found. Hodgins tried not to think how that would have smelled. The cause of death was stabbing. The knife was still in the body when they found him. It was assumed to be from the kitchen as it matched other knives found there.

Olivia had been bludgeoned to death with a piece of firewood, as well as having her throat slit. They hadn't found the knife. *Were they all weapons of convenience? Could it be possible the same person committed both crimes after all?*

Hodgins slid over the pad of paper he'd been writing on earlier. He added a few more things about his case, and added points from Carter's file. There were a few similarities.

Both places showed signs of a struggle, and the

weapons seems to be found conveniently at the homes by the killer. Did someone break in intending only theft? Carter had no leads, except a vague description from a neighbour. She had heard yelling a few days earlier and saw a man running from the house. She couldn't provide much of a description, only that he was tall and bulky.

Hodgins realized he had no idea what Webster looked like. Only knew his age. He'd have to remedy that. Miss O'Hara could help. He pulled out his pocket watch and checked the time. Cordelia would be expecting him home soon, and he was too tired to go back to Duchess Street. He'd speak with Miss O'Hara tomorrow. Maybe he'd just send Barnes instead. Hodgins tore the sheet from the pad and pinned it up next to the other pages before heading home.

CHAPTER 15

The high temperatures were back and Hodgins woke feeling sticky and uncomfortable. He turned towards the window. It was open but the curtains were still. He threw back the sheets and swung his legs over the side of the bed. Using the sleeve of his dressing gown, he wiped the beads of sweat from his brow, then pushed himself off the bed.

Cordelia stirred but did not wake. Hodgins tiptoed to the dressing table and splashed his face with the water from the basin. The water was tepid, but it felt good. He attended to his morning routine, dressed, and went down to the kitchen.

It was quite early, but he couldn't sleep. He tore a chunk of bread from yesterday's loaf, smeared some peach jelly on it and wrote a short note for Cordelia before heading to the station.

It was far too early for the trolley so he walked. He noticed how quiet it was outside – the birds were still in bed. His steps were slower than usual, partially due to the heat and partially because he was deep in thought. The quiet helped him mentally organize all he knew about the girl's death.

That salesman, Webster, might've had something to do with Olivia's death. He had been bothering her and she spurned his attentions. Webster stayed at the boarding house often enough to know the neighbourhood and the residents. He conveniently left town before her body was discovered. Coincidence? And Webster has a reputation with young women.

Hodgins had no proof and no other suspects. Damn inconvenient of the man to be on the road when Hodgins desperately needed to talk to him. He kicked a pebble and watched it bounce out into the road.

When he arrived at the station it was just as quiet as the rest of the neighbourhood. There was hardly anyone there, and those present were trying to stay cool. The only sounds were from paper being fanned and the occasional yawn. He noticed a few uniforms with the top button open, but he didn't say anything. He hadn't bothered to do up his top button either.

He went into the back and automatically made a cup of tea, then went into his office and wrote down some ideas he had.

As soon as Barnes came in Hodgins sent him off to

get Webster's description while he went in search of Dr. McKenzie. The whistling coming from inside the coroner's office let Hodgins know he was in.

"And what can I do for you this bonnie morning Detective?"

"Do you recall the details of the painter's autopsy? Any similarities between that and Olivia Nolan?"

McKenzie tugged at his bushy red whiskers. "Nothing I can recall. Let me check my records." McKenzie retrieved the two files and spread the papers across an empty autopsy table.

"One stabbed, one beaten. Neither body had any unusually markings on them. What makes you think they could be connected?"

"Nothing really. Just that both murders happened only a block apart and only a couple of weeks between them. Grasping at straws I suppose."

Hodgins looked over McKenzie's shoulder at the reports. "Nothing on the clothing?"

"Only blood and paint on the painter, and blood and bits of wood on the girl. I was going over her clothing again yesterday just before I left." He pointed towards an evidence box. "Had one of the constables bring that over late yesterday afternoon. Was going to see you today as a matter of fact. I found one black strand of hair on her clothing, and she has auburn hair. Don't know how I missed it."

"What about the painter? Any black hairs on him?"

"He had black hair himself, so yes, there were black hairs on him. No way to tell for certain if they were his or not. Took a look under the 'scope and they seemed similar, so I imagine the hairs on his clothing were his own. The strand I took off the wee lassie will be in the evidence box. I can show you the comparison between the girl's and the ones from the painter if you'd like. Don't know what good it'll do if they're different though. No way to tell where they would have come from."

"I'd be interested to see them. Even if I can't find out where the hair came from, it might just connect the two."

Hodgins watched as McKenzie took the hair from the evidence box with Olivia's belongings and placed it on a microscope slide. McKenzie had two microscopes sitting side by side on his table. He put the hair from the painter under the other. He looked at one, then the other, then back to the first one. He refocused the scopes and went back and forth between them several more times before turning to Hodgins.

"See for yourself. Don't believe they came from the same person. The hair found on the painter is thick and course. The one from Olivia's clothing is in much better condition. Left by someone who took care of his appearance I'd say. The strand off her clothing is longer and has a bit of a wave too."

"So nothing to connect the two then? Blast." Hodgins thanked McKenzie for his time before turning and heading back to the station.

Barnes arrived about fifteen minutes later.

"Well?" Hodgins asked.

"Got a right good description of Mr. Webster. He's got longish black hair, 'bout to his shoulders, beard and moustache, green eyes, slender and round about six foot tall."

Hodgins drummed his fingers on the desk top. "Could be."

"Could be what, Sir?"

"That painter that was killed over on Duke Street near the beginning of the month. A neighbour saw a tall man running away. Said he was bulky, but if it was dark and he was running I don't suppose she could really tell how heavy he was. Bulky could just mean he was muscular."

"But Miss O'Hara said Webster was slender."

"She just may have meant he wasn't fat. Blast. He won't be back in Toronto for days yet. It seems he comes here every two weeks. That would put him here when the painter was killed too. I wish there was a way to get in touch with people right away, no matter where they were."

"That would be nice, but I can't see that happening, Sir. Rather unrealistic don't you think?"

Hodgins sighed. "You're right. Silly idea really."

"But why kill a painter?"

Hodgins looked past Barnes. "Finally."

"Sir?"

Hodgins pointed towards the door and Barnes turned to look. Kendall Nolan had just come in and walked over to the sergeant's desk. The sergeant pointed to Hodgins. Nolan waved and walked over.

"Talk to the lads who worked with Carter. Find out if the painter had a wife or lady friend. Webster has a reputation," Hodgins said.

Barnes hesitated and watched as Nolan approached.

"Off with you. Now."

"Yes, Sir." Barnes nodded at Nolan as they passed, and went to talk with the other constables as Hodgins greeted Nolan.

"Mr. Nolan, you're a hard man to find." Hodgins wanted to yell at the man, but held his tongue. "Have a seat. I went up to Woodbridge twice but no one seemed to know where to find you. Finally tracked down someone who directed me to Pine Grove."

Nolan paled. "You . . . You were in Pine Grove?"

"Yes. Was even given directions to your farm."

"You went to the farm?" Nolan whispered.

"No. Man who gave me the directions said you'd just left town a bit earlier. Didn't see any point riding out, what with you not being there and all."

Nolan seemed relieved and his colour returned.

"Tell me, how does a man of your means afford two homes? I gather the one in Pine Grove is a fair size. The farms I passed all seemed quite large."

"Inheritance. Why were you looking for me? Have you found the man who killed Olivia?" Nolan moved forward in the chair and grasped the edge of the desk. "When can I bury her? She should be with her mother now."

"Dr. McKenzie has been ready to release her for several days. We were waiting for you to show up."

Hodgins thought he sounded a little sharp, but he just didn't like Nolan. It was nothing he could put his finger on, but ever since Nolan rushed out of the city he had a bad feeling about him.

"Is something the matter?" Nolan asked.

Hodgins realized that he was staring at Nolan's hair. Blonde. Hodgins figured the girl got her colouring from her mother. He didn't really believe he had killed his own daughter, but anything was possible.

"No, just thinking. If you leave me the details, I'll

make sure your daughter's body is sent wherever you'd like."

Nolan blanched when Hodgins mentioned his daughter's body. Hodgins felt sorry for the man, understanding how he must feel. He just couldn't comprehend Nolan's actions though.

Nolan wrote down the name of the church on a page that Hodgins had torn from his notebook.

"I suppose I'd better speak with the vicar over at St. James and make the arrangements." He slid the paper over to Hodgins. "My late wife Ruth loved the chapel there."

CHAPTER 16

When Nolan left, Hodgins went over to Barnes' desk. "Don't suppose you came across anything about an inheritance? Nolan claims that's how he got the farm."

"No, nothing like that. Could be in a local rag though."

Hodgins sighed. "Nothing is coming together on this one. You keep looking here. I'll go back to Woodbridge and Pine Grove and ask around some more."

Hodgins went back to his office and looked through the desk drawers for the train schedule. It had been shoved to the back of a drawer and was stuck in a tiny crack in the wood. He wiggled it around, trying not to tear it. He only lost one small corner. He ran his finger down the page checking the times. *Too late for the morning train.* He'd have to wait until one. Wouldn't give him much time if he wanted to get the last train back as there weren't very many going back and forth.

With Barnes and a few of the lads checking on Nolan

and time to kill before the train left, Hodgins decided to take a side trip to a bookstore after lunch. With all the plans his wife had for a garden, Hodgins realized they would need help.

Neither had gardened before as his mother-in-law wouldn't allow them near *her* precious garden. He figured there must be books on the subject.

There was a book seller on King Street which was on his way to Union Station.

Cordelia had packed up some of the remnants of last evenings meal so he had a good lunch before leaving. A bit of cold beef, a chunk of bread and one of her delicious strawberry tarts. She even thought to include a linen napkin. He spread it out on his desk and placed his food on top, then went to the back room and made another cup of tea.

As he stood by his desk munching away and reading over the sheets he had pinned to the wall, he made a list of suspects. It was very short. William Howland, President of the Board of Trade. *Already eliminated.* John Webster, salesman. *Undecided.* Kendall Nolan. *Is he really a suspect?* Hodgins put a question marked beside his name. And what about the missing woman and the dead painter? Were they connected? He circled the last two.

Hodgins had a few ideas running through his mind,

but nothing concrete. He needed more information. Finishing his lunch, he left the station and walked down Parliament to King, turning west. He found the shop of Rowsell and Hutching just past Church Street.

A little bell tinkled as Hodgins opened the door. There was no one in sight. *What's the point of the blasted bell when no one comes to help?* He wandered around looking at the books and stationery items, not really certain what he was after.

"May I be of assistance Sir?"

Hodgins looked up. *Where did he come from?* A middle aged man approached. He was undoubtedly the thinnest man Hodgins had come across. A strong gust of wind would probably blow him clear across Lake Ontario.

"I find myself in need of a book on flowers and such. We've just moved and the gardens have been frightfully neglected. I don't know where to start. I thought there might be a book?"

The man's eyes lit up and he clapped his hands. "Oh, I have just the thing. Imported from England. They have the most magnificent gardens there, don't you know. Follow me."

He scampered towards the back and behind a tall bookshelf. Hodgins followed. He walked behind the shelf and watched the clerk running his fingers along the spines of the books.

"Ah, here it is. *The Gardener – A Magazine of Horticulture and Floriculture.* It's by David Thomson." He spoke the author's name with reverence. Hodgins assumed he must be an expert. The clerk handed him the book.

Hodgins was surprised by the size and weight. He flipped to the end. Almost 600 pages.

"A magazine?"

"Yes, rather a misleading name, isn't it? It's a new publication, 1873. Quite modern." The clerk spoke about the book and the author, extolling his many qualities.

Hodgins thumbed through the book while the clerk nattered on, and came across a page with the heading *Hints for Amateurs*.

"I'll take it. Would you be good enough to hold it for me until the end of the day?"

The clerk looked doubtful. "Well, I don't know . . ."

"I'm Detective Albert Hodgins." He pulled out his badge. "I assure you I will return for it. I'll pay in advance."

The clerk smiled. "Detective you say? Of course. I'll be happy to put it aside for you."

Hodgins paid for the book and checked his pocket watch. He'd spent more time in the store than he thought, as the clerk had prattled on about the book. He had to hurry to the train station or he'd miss his chance to go to

Woodbridge today.

Hodgins settled into a seat near the rear of the passenger car and dozed off. The windows were all down and the wind whistled though the car keeping him from a deep sleep.

He opened his eyes when he heard the conductor shouting, "Woodbridge, next stop Woodbridge" as he walked through the train.

As soon as he got into town he walked to the livery, hired a buggy again, and headed to Pine Grove. He stopped at the general store as that seemed to be the only place he was able to get information. He wanted to see if he could find out anything further about Nolan. The store owner recognized him.

"Good afternoon, Detective. Still looking for Mr. Nolan?

"No. I spoke to him this morning. He mentioned something that got me wondering. Do you know who previously owned his farm?"

"Matter of fact I do. Used to belong to my brother."

"Your brother?" Hodgins was puzzled. "You're related to Nolan?"

He shook his head. "Whatever gave you that idea? No, no. My brother decided to try his hand farming out west. Just got it into his head one day it was better farming out there."

"Must have misunderstood. I thought he got the farm from a relative." He took his notebook out of his jacket pocket and jotted down what he just learned. "Unfortunate about his daughter."

"Daughter? They have no children." The store owner laughed. "I do believe we're talking about two different people."

Hodgins nodded. "Could be. Nolan is in his forties, balding slightly, average height, stocky but not fat. Sells pharmaceuticals."

"Yes, that's Mr. Nolan, but he doesn't have a daughter."

"Strange. Won't keep you from your customers any longer." He tipped his hat and went back to the buggy.

He sat thinking for a moment. He noticed the store owner kept saying they, as though Nolan's wife was still alive. He decided to look for the farm even though Nolan was still in Toronto.

Hodgins remembered the directions he was given from the last visit. If he followed the road east, he should find it.

Hodgins cursed at the beast pulling the buggy. The horse was being quite temperamental. It didn't seem to matter if he was gentle or relied heavily on the whip. The horse went at a pace it was comfortable with, completely unconcerned with what Hodgins wanted.

He counted the farms as he passed them, and he was finally at a laneway heading to the third one. A small white house sat at the end of the long lane, with a barn farther back on the property. It didn't appear that Nolan was growing any crops, but he spotted a fair sized vegetable garden out front of the house.

He drove the buggy up and a woman in her early thirties came out to greet him. Hodgins thought she might be a housekeeper, but something told him otherwise. *Too well dressed.* He took a chance.

"Mrs. Nolan?"

"Ya, I'm Mrs. Nolan."

"Mrs. Kendall Nolan?"

"Ya. Do ya know my husband? 'Fraid he ain't here. Won't be back for several days."

Hodgins showed his badge. Mrs. Nolan took one look at it and fainted.

CHAPTER 17

Hodgins leapt off the buggy and ran to her side. He lifted her and placed her in the rocker on the porch, out of the sun. As the clerk in town had commented, she was pretty, but he noticed deep lines around her eyes, and she wore a lot of make-up. *Unusual for a farm wife.* She started to come around.

"Are you ill? I can take you into town to the doctor." Hodgins didn't even know if there was a doctor in Pine Grove.

She waved him away. "Must be this blasted heat."

"I only wanted to inquire about your husband. I have a few questions. But if you're not feeling well . . ."

She look relieved, as though she'd expected him to say something else. *Funny. Nolan had seemed relieved when I told him I hadn't gone out to the farm.* At least now he knew why.

"What did ya wanna know?" She leaned forward and spit out a small wad of chewing tobacco.

Hodgins raised an eyebrow as he pulled out his trusty notebook and thumbed through the pages.

"How long have you been married?"

"A little over four years."

"You bought the farm shortly after?"

"Ya. Ain't no law a'gin it. Why ya interested in my husband and our marriage?"

"Do you know where he stays when he's in Toronto?"

She shrugged her shoulders. "Boarding house or hotel I expect." She bit her bottom lip. She wasn't telling him everything, but he let it go, for now.

"There was a murder on the street where he stays. Did he mention it?"

She eyed him suspiciously. "If'n ya already know where he stays, why'd ya ask me?"

"Just checking, in case he stayed at more than one place."

She didn't seem all that upset or shocked. "He's bin rather upset the past few days. Didn't want to talk about it. That must be why."

"Hmmm. Must be." He turned to a clean page and made some notes. When he looked up at her again, she was tapping her fingers on the arms of the rocker, and she still seemed pale.

"Are you sure you don't want me to take you to town?"

"No, I'll just sit here in the shade. I'm fine."

Hodgins stood, thanked her for her time and went back to Pine Grove. He had noticed a couple of churches earlier as he went through town. He stopped at the first one, looking for a record of the marriage. He wasn't even sure they were married there, or even married at all.

A quick chat with the vicar and he left without any information. He went to the next one and found what he was looking for.

The minister had a record of the marriage. Hodgins copied down the details from the registry and drove the horse hard in order to make the last train. When he got back to Toronto, he remembered to stop and pick up his gardening book before going home.

* * *

After dinner Sara went out into the back yard to play with Scraps, and Cordelia and Hodgins went out to the back porch to watch. The previous owners had left a large bench behind, too heavy to move. It needed a new coat of paint but was quite sturdy. Cordelia took the opportunity to ask about the murder.

"You won't believe it," he told her. "Never in your wildest dreams can you guess what I found out today." He leaned back grinning. "Go ahead. Guess."

"Since I haven't a clue what you're referring to I won't even try. What have you found out?"

"Nolan has another wife."

"So? Lots of people remarry."

He leaned forward. "No, you don't understand. His wife died a year or so ago. This wife has been around for over four years."

Cordelia's hand flew to her mouth. "No!"

"Yes. Bad enough the man's lost his daughter. Now I have to arrest him for bigamy. Interesting woman though. Rather rough, if you know what I mean. Even chews tobacco."

Cordelia tisked.

"Think I'll wait until after he buries Olivia. It's not like he knows that I found out. His wife, the second one, isn't expecting him for several days. He's making burial arrangements today, so his daughter will be laid to rest before he goes back up. I'll bet anything one of the neighbours will have something arranged for after the service and funeral. Can't imagine he'll be able to go back to Pine Grove until the next morning so I'll catch him first thing. The service is over at St. Andrew's. Maybe tomorrow afternoon I'll wander over and see what the arrangements are."

"You don't think it's possible he killed his daughter so he could live with his new wife, do you?" Cordelia asked, then thought for a moment. "Could he have killed his first wife?"

"Now that's interesting. He married the second one four years ago. His first wife just died last year. Maybe he got tired of juggling them."

It was getting dark so they called Sara in. Hodgins went down the hall and picked his jacket off the post at the end of the upstairs railing where he had draped it. Retrieving his notebook and pencil from the pocket, he went into the sitting room and sat on the edge of the chair. Resting the notebook on his knee, he mumbled as he wrote.

"Check out the first wife. How did she die? Was she ill long or was it sudden?" He glanced up as Cordelia came in.

"Good thinking Delia. Personally I don't believe the man has it in him to plan a murder, but one never knows."

He propped his elbow on the arm of the chair and tapped his lips with the pencil.

"Wonder if either of the women knew about the other?"

"Is it possible the second wife did in the first?"

Hodgins looked shocked for a moment, then laughed. "Really Delia. Where do you pick up such things? 'Did in' indeed. However . . ." He paused to mull it over. "Woman have been known to commit murder. Usually poison or some such thing. Can't imagine a woman chasing a girl and bashing her head in with a piece of firewood."

He noticed his wife pale slightly. "Sorry Dear. Guess those stories you read aren't quite as gruesome as real life."

"It's not that. I was just thinking about Sara. How horrible it must have been to find his daughter like that."

Before Hodgins could respond, the back door slammed. He heard the hurried clicking of Scraps' claws on the floor. The dog turned into the room, sliding into the door frame as he went. He ran to Hodgins and put his big hairy front paws on his lap. Hodgins pushed him down and tried to wipe the mud off his trousers.

"Guess not everything has dried up yet." The dog sat in front of him, mouth open, tongue hanging off to the side. His tail thumped on the floor.

Sara came in holding a towel. "Sorry Daddy. He ran past me when I let him in. I tried to grab him to clean all the mud off his feet, but he was too fast."

"You just had to have a dog. Should've found a smaller one." Cordelia smiled and got up. "Guess I'd better clean the floor. Sara, give your father the towel so he can get some of the mud off, then grab that dog and come help me."

CHAPTER 18

Since Hodgins had the day off, he slept in for the first time since his short trip to Kingston. *Could get used to this.*

When he finally went downstairs, Sara had already finished breakfast and gone to visit a friend for the day. Scraps picked himself up from his spot beside the icebox and went to greet Hodgins. He was rewarded with a good scratch behind the ears.

Cordelia, having heard him move about, was busy preparing their breakfast. He kissed her on the cheek then took the kettle off the stove. He made two cups of tea, one black, one sweet for his wife. Cordelia placed a jar of her peach jelly on the table, then served up the eggs and sausages. When she brought over the fresh-baked bread she finally sat down.

"What do you have planned for today?" he asked.

Cordelia took a sip of tea. "I think I'll go over to Mother's this morning and see if I can't finish up the draperies today."

"Can't that wait a bit? I haven't seen much of you this week. Thought we could spend the morning together. Maybe tackle the weeds in the garden? It'll be much too hot in the afternoon."

Cordelia took a bite of her eggs, considering what to do. "Well, I suppose the drapes can wait until next week. It would be nice to start on the garden. Give the poor flowers a chance to grow. Maybe we can clear a space for vegetables? If I plant some beets, broccoli and turnips, they'll be ready for fall."

Hodgins looked at his pocket watch and smiled.

"I bought quite a large book on gardening yesterday. It'll take all winter to read it."

"Yes, I saw it on the small table in the front room. I was looking through it and saw a chapter on vegetables for winter and spring."

"Need to buy some tools. I'll do that once we've finished breakfast. One of the hardware stores on King should have hoes, rakes, and the like. Paterson & Son maybe, or Rice Lewis."

They finished their breakfast, chatting about what they wanted or needed to do in their garden. Hodgins had grabbed a piece of paper and pencil and started making a list. He left Cordelia cleaning up the kitchen and rushed off to buy the necessary garden tools. He wanted to get back and start working on the gardens before they got sidetracked. If he didn't keep busy, Cordelia would know something was up as he'd just be pacing around looking at his pocket watch all morning. He couldn't wait to see her reaction.

Hodgins found what he had on his list, plus a few other items the clerk suggested would be useful. He had hired a buggy as he knew he would end up with far more than he could handle.

With the tools in the back yard and buggy returned, Cordelia set about restoring the gardens. After changing into the pair of denims the clerk had recommended, and an old shirt, Hodgins was ready to tackle the pathetic garden along the front porch. He left Cordelia in the backyard with Scraps, marking out an area for her vegetables. There was already a small patch, but it wasn't near large enough to suit her.

Hodgins went out front with his new trowel and wheelbarrow. Since he hadn't thought about buying one of those before he left, he was more than glad he rented the buggy. He positioned the wheelbarrow within easy reach, got down on his knees and went about digging up weeds.

He was pretty certain he could tell the different and not dig up any flowers. At least not enough that anyone would notice. He managed to get about half-way through the garden to the left of the porch steps when the delivery man arrived. Cordelia was still in the back. Hodgins helped the man put it in the room off the kitchen. Fortunately Cordelia was facing away from the house and couldn't see them struggling with it, and Scraps was sleeping under a tree. He would have raised a fuss if he saw Hodgins moving about.

The room was going to be a pantry, but it was big enough to double as a sewing room. At least for the time being. There were a few unpacked boxes in the corner, and a small table that Hodgins had snuck in the night before.

He made sure the machine was set up so Cordelia could look out the window. It would also provide her with more light than the lantern would. He hadn't thought about a chair, but she could use one from the kitchen.

As soon as the delivery man left, Hodgins went out to fetch Cordelia.

He kept his hand on the door so it wouldn't bang shut. Keeping one eye on the dog, he crept across the yard, ensuring neither his wife nor the dog heard him. Cordelia was standing, surveying the area she had marked off. Hodgins reached up and placed his hands over her eyes. Scraps woke up when she screamed.

"Hush, you'll have the neighbour's thinking I beat my wife."

"What are you up to Bertie?"

Scraps ran over, barking and jumping, trying to get in on the game.

"Come with me." Hodgins turned her towards the house and stood behind her, making sure he kept his hands over her eyes. "Just walk straight. I'll tell you when we reach the porch."

She took a few steps and stumbled as Scraps jumped in front of her. Hodgins grabbed her, laughing. He allowed her to go as far as the porch before covering her eyes again.

He took one hand away to open the door and held it with his foot. The dog scampered in. With her eyes firmly covered, he guided her through the kitchen and into the side room. Scraps ran ahead to investigate what was behind the door that had always been closed. Hodgins removed his hands from her eyes.

"Oh my, it's beautiful." She went over and ran her hands across the machine. She traced the gold scrolling with her finger. The colour sparkled against the jet black case of the machine. She turned the hand crank a few times before turning back to Hodgins.

"This looks brand new. How can we afford such a thing? Really, you shouldn't have . . . but I'm glad you did." She ran over and threw her arms around his neck.

"No more trips to Mother's to use her old machine. She'll be so jealous."

"I'll have to get you a chair for it, and I can put up some more shelves. Anything you need, let me know."

She took a step back. "Are you certain we can afford it? A used machine will do just as well."

"Don't worry. I got a good discount from the dealer."

There was a knock on the front door and Scraps went tearing down the hall, tail wagging, barking all the way.

"What else have you been spending our money on?" Cordelia stood with her hands on her hips.

Hodgins put his hands up in front of him. "I swear I haven't bought anything else."

Hodgins called the dog and Cordelia put Scraps in the backyard. Hodgins opened the front door to an embarrassed looking Barnes, holding a covered plate in his hands. Hodgins raised an eyebrow.

"What's this?"

"Um, my mother baked you something. Says a gift of fresh-baked bread to welcome someone to a new house is good luck or some such thing. She wanted to give you a few weeks to settle in." Barnes shrugged. "May your family never know hunger."

"That's very nice of her. It smells wonderful. Why didn't you bring her along?"

"Said she didn't want to impose."

"So she sent you to impose instead."

Barnes eyes grew wide. "Sir, I didn't mean to intrude." He thrust the plate into Hodgins chest and stepped back.

Hodgins laughed and took the plate. "I was only joking with you. You and your family are always welcome here." He looked over Barnes shoulder and pointed. "You might want to find more excuses to drop in on your days off."

Barnes turned around and saw a middle-age couple walking up the path to the house next door, followed by a young woman in her twenties.

"Oh, she's the most beautiful girl I've ever seen." Barnes stood gaping, his lower jaw slowly dropping farther and farther down.

The man spotted them, waved, then cut across the lawn towards them. "Hello neighbour."

"Good day Mr. Halloway."

"Who's this fine young man?" he asked, thrusting his fleshy hand toward Barnes.

"Mr. Halloway, this is Henry Barnes. He's one of my constables."

Halloway shook Barnes' hand vigorously, pumping it up and down several times. "Constable, eh? So you have a steady job. Good. Good."

Barnes gave Hodgins a puzzled look and shrugged. "Hello Mr. Halloway. Nice to meet you."

"Oh, and manners too. Very good, very good."

"Barnes has ambitions to become a detective, and he's quite good. Won't be long before he out ranks me," Hodgins remarked.

"Very good, very good. Are you married young man?"

"Um, no Sir."

"Good looking lad like you? Sweetheart?"

Barnes turned deeper shades of red with each question. "No Sir, no sweetheart."

Halloway reached out and straightened Barnes' tie. "Good looking, snappy dresser, well groomed, fit by the looks of you. Quite the catch."

Hodgins decided to rescue Barnes from further interrogation. "I'm afraid we have to go Halloway. My wife's been anxiously awaiting this bread. She'll have my hide if I stay and yabber on too long."

"Quite right, quite right. I know what you mean." Halloway winked. "My missus is the same. Nice to meet you young man. Hope to see you again." He turned and strolled back to his house and Hodgins ushered Barnes inside.

"He's trying to marry off his daughter. Seems he's taken a liking to you."

"That's was very embarrassing, I don't mind saying. But his daughter is quite breathtaking."

"Come in and say hello to Cordelia. She'll want to thank you and your mother for the bread. Scraps will want to say hello too."

CHAPTER 19

Barnes' only stayed long enough to say hello to Cordelia and have a little rough and tumble with Scraps in the backyard. While he was doing that, Cordelia wrote out a thank you note to his mother. Barnes took the note and hurried off home. Hodgins noticed Barnes looking over at the house next door, probably hoping for a glimpse of the daughter again.

Hodgins went into the backyard to see what Cordelia had been doing while he had worked out front. She had marked off an area at least ten foot square, right in the middle of the lawn. The old shabby looking garden was still there, but Cordelia had expanded it on all sides. She had roped off an area with sticks and twine, all ready for Hodgins to start to digging.

"Rather large, isn't it? For broccoli, beets, and turnip I mean."

"Come spring I want to plant all sorts of vegetables. If we dig it up now, there will be less to do in the spring. I'll only plant a few rows now."

"Good thinking. Probably be all muddy and wet in the spring. Don't relish the thought of digging then."

Hodgins looked around the yard, stopping at the large maple on the east side.

"You know what might be nice? A shelter for the dog. Already got a fence around the property so he can run around. Might be nice to have a small place for him to go if it starts to rain. Can't be too difficult to build. Just four walls and a roof. Right under that tree. He seems to like it there anyway." He took another look at the large dog.

"Well, reasonably small."

"Before you get too carried away, why don't we have some lunch? It's getting too hot to do much more anyway."

They both changed into clean clothes and Cordelia prepared a light meal. Once they finished, Hodgins helped clean up. She gathered up her fabric and dragged a kitchen chair into her new sewing room to work on the draperies. Hodgins went over to St. James Cathedral to speak with Reverend Mitchell.

"Sorry to disturb you, but I was just wondering what arrangements have been made for Olivia Nolan. I understand her father wished to have the service here."

"Yes, he came in yesterday. How sad to lose one's child. She was such a nice girl. Came in often with her mother. Mr. Nolan was not a regular church goer, but Mrs. Nolan was quite devoted. The service for Olivia will be tomorrow afternoon at two."

"Do you know where she will be buried?"

"Mrs. Nolan is buried in our cemetery up on Parliament. Olivia is to be laid to rest beside her."

Hodgins reached out to shake the Reverend's hand. "Thank you for your time."

Hodgins was thinking about the death of the first Mrs. Nolan, and without even realizing it, he headed off in the direction of the cemetery. A half hour later he entered through the large black wrought iron gates on the east side of Parliament Street. He had no idea where Mrs. Nolan was buried or why he even came to the cemetery, but it was a pleasant spot with a nice view.

Hodgins was immediately drawn to the chapel off to his left, up on a small hill. The spire at the front was noticeable from quite a distance and he had been curious about it before, but never had the time to check it out. He went part way up the walk then veered onto the grass and circled around.

The chapel was magnificent from every angle. The cemetery was nestled among the trees, making it feel much cooler than it was. Hodgins could hear the roar of the water from the Don River somewhere off to the east. He turned back and walked around the north side, and circled back towards the entrance. He wandered around looking at some of the headstones, wondering what had happened to the people, especially the young ones.

Hearing a sound up ahead, he followed it. Two men were digging a grave. He walked over. The men looked up, nodded and kept digging. Hodgins looked at the headstones by the grave being dug. The one on the right had Ruth Nolan's name on it. He had found Olivia's final resting place.

He was on duty Sunday, but the cemetery was only a twenty minute walk from the station on Wilton. He thought he would attend the service, and had a feeling Barnes might wish to join him.

Hodgins had already planned to wait until Monday to confront Nolan about his two wives and arrest him for bigamy, so he would keep his distance at the cemetery. Since he thought Nolan might move up to Pine Grove, Hodgins checked the train schedule to make sure he was at the house on Duchess well before Nolan could leave to catch the first train to Woodbridge.

Hodgins looked at a few more graves and found the marker for Reverend James Fielding, the fourth Bishop of Toronto. It was a large but simple stone, in the shape of a cross. Since there was nothing for him to do at the cemetery, he headed back home.

* * *

Scraps was still in the yard, but he had moved from under the maple as the sun had shifted the shade. He had wiggled under a bush in the back corner and fallen asleep. Hodgins called him and he came running into the kitchen and straight to his water bowl. *We'll have to put a bowl outside for him.* Scraps flopped down beside the ice box and Hodgins went into the sewing room to see how Cordelia was enjoying her new machine. She hummed as she sewed.

"Works ok then?"

"Oh yes. It sews so smoothly." She stopped at the end of the seam and reached down to her side.

"I've got one complete set done already." She held up some chintz curtains. "I'll have them all done by the end of next week I'm sure."

"Room's a little drab, don't you think?" He asked. "Maybe some wallpaper?"

"Plenty of time for that. I'm just happy I don't have to carry the fabric back and forth to Mother's all the time. I wouldn't mind a work table though. I'm certain we can find a second hand one somewhere."

Sara came home in time for dinner, her dress dirty around the bottom, with a blue stains down the front.

"What ever have you been in to?" Cordelia asked.

"We went picking berries. See?"

Sara held out a small cloth-covered basket. Cordelia lifted the cloth, revealing a basket full of blueberries.

"May I bake a blueberry pie tomorrow? Please?"

"Yes, after breakfast you can help me bake a pie. Now go upstairs, change into a clean dress, and bring that one down so I can try to get those stains out, then I'll show you what your father bought."

She took the basket from Sara and sent her upstairs.

CHAPTER 20

Hodgins stood in front of Barnes' desk. "Have you found out anything about that woman in Pine Grove?"

"Yes, it seems she has a bit of a record. Nothin' big. Petty theft mostly. How could a man like Nolan get mixed up with someone like that?"

"Who knows? What else do we know about her?"

"Full name's Mary Elizabeth Cooper. Hails from Buffalo near as I can tell. I sent a telegram down Friday. Got a reply Saturday saying they were sending some information up on the train. Just waiting for it to arrive. Hopefully it comes today, or at least by Monday."

"Let me know the moment it arrives."

Hodgins went into his office, but found himself at loose ends. *Maybe if I take my mind off it for a bit.*

He pulled the pad of foolscap out and started sketching. Trying to assess the size of his dog, he added figures to the drawing. Scraps head was about waist high. The doghouse needed to be tall enough for the dog to stand. He was finishing up a very detailed drawing when the church bells rang, signalling the eleven o'clock service. He folded the paper, slipped it into his pocket, and went back to reviewing the case.

Hodgins had been so immersed in sorting out the details, he missed lunch. He unwrapped the leftovers that Cordelia had packed and ate hurriedly. Hunger satisfied, he stepped outside his office.

"Barnes."

Barnes came rushing out from the back, spilling his tea. "Yes, Sir?"

"How'd you like to attend a funeral?"

Barnes stared blankly

"Olivia Nolan is being buried today. Thought you'd want to tag along."

Barnes put the teacup down on Hodgins' desk "Yes, Sir. Very much."

"Come along then. The service at the church should be over. Expect they'll be taking her up to St. James Cemetery 'bout now."

They left the station and turned up Parliament. The procession was a few blocks ahead of them. Picking up their pace, they soon fell in step with the people at the back. Hodgins recognized the Green's and McGregor's. He though he spotted Miss O'Hara a little farther up.

143

"Quite a few older children," Barnes commented.

"Natural, I expect. She probably had a lot of friends. Everyone seemed to like the girl."

Once they arrived at the cemetery, Hodgins knew exactly where to go. He grabbed Barnes by the arm and pulled him off the roadway.

"Over here."

They cut across the grass and stood far enough from the open grave to be out of the way, but close enough they could easily observe everyone. Hodgins also did not want to intrude. A child's funeral was always more sombre.

The adults were quiet – no one seemed to want to speak. Several of Olivia's friends were crying. The sound carried through the quiet cemetery. They quieted down a bit once Reverend Mitchell started to speak.

"Sir," Barnes whispered. "Have you noticed Miss O'Hara? She's the only neighbour keeping her distance from Mr. Nolan. Before the preacher started, everyone approached him. Everyone except her."

"Yes, I did notice that. She actually looks a little guilty. Hasn't really spoken to many, and those she did speak with, she didn't look in the eye."

The grave-side service ended and Hodgins nudged Barnes. "Look. Miss O'Hara is scampering off."

They watched as she hurried out of the cemetery.

Everyone else lingered, paying their respects. A few went inside the chapel. Mrs. Green turned around and saw them standing off to the side. She spoke to her husband, then approached them.

"Nice of you to attend. You're welcome to come back to our house. I'm sure Mr. Nolan would appreciate that."

Hodgins noticed that she was much calmer now. A nice change from the hysterical women he met earlier.

"Thank you," Hodgins said, "but we have things to attend to."

She started to leave, then turned back. "Do you know who did it?

Both men shook their heads.

"Thought maybe if ya did, he might change his mind about moving." She turned and joined her husband by the grave.

"I knew it," Hodgins said. "He's going to go live with the second wife. First thing tomorrow you and I are going to his house to arrest him. Don't want him getting on the first train out. You can take him back to the station and I'll have another chat with Miss O'Hara. She knows something."

They made their way back to the station on Wilton Street and the desk sergeant called Hodgins over as soon as they stepped through the door.

"There's a copper from New York what came in a short while ago. He's in with Chief Draper now. A Captain Harrison."

"Hmm. Must be about Mary Cooper. Wonder why a captain was sent up?"

Hodgins was telling Barnes about their visitor when Draper came out of his office with the Captain. He called Hodgins over.

"This is Captain Thomas Harrison, New York Police. Got some interesting news about your Mary Cooper."

Draper turned to Harrison. "Detective Hodgins is handling this one. I'll leave you in his capable hands."

The Chief went back to his office and left Hodgins and Harrison to talk.

Hodgins took Harrison into his office and gestured towards the chair opposite his desk.

"What brings you up here? We were expecting information to be sent, not a Captain."

"We've been looking for Mary Cooper for five years. She's a person of interest if you will. Her husband died under mysterious circumstances. While the autopsy was being done, she scarpered. Turns out he was poisoned. We think she either done him in herself, or got some poor slob to do it for her."

Harrison leaned on the desk towards Hodgins. "Did

she murder another husband up here?"

"No. Maybe. I don't know. She's married, and her husband's child from his first marriage was just murdered. We're going to arrest him tomorrow for bigamy."

"Well I never. Murdered a child? Wouldn't have thought that of her. Didn't seem the sort. Ya just never can tell. Bigamist husband you say. Interesting case you got there."

"She's not at the top of my list of suspects, but she is on it. I don't even know if she knew about the first wife. After we arrest Mr. Nolan, the man she married, I plan on taking the first train up to where they're living. About an hour's ride. You're more than welcome to accompany me. We can both question her."

Hodgins thought for a moment. "I guess you have seniority, so to speak. If she is a suspect in the murder of her husband in New York, you'll have to take her back for trial. If we find her guilty, you can send her back up to us when you're through with her. If you don't hang her first." He pulled out his notebook.

"I'll fill you in on everything here. You may as well stay a few days, if that's agreeable with you. Toronto has many fine establishments."

Hodgins called Barnes over and the three of them spent the next few hours reviewing all the information they had, and tossing around ideas until the end of the day.

Harrison left to go back to his hotel. Hodgins and Barnes went home.

* * *

Once their evening meal was eaten, the kitchen cleaned up, and Sara put to bed, Hodgins and Cordelia settled into their chairs in the front room. They always sat in the same two chairs; his a simple arm chair, hers the settee. She frequently had sewing or needlework spread out, or Sara snuggled in close. Hodgins picked his gardening book off the end table and notice a few pieces of paper sticking out from between the pages.

"What's this?"

"I was looking through it earlier and found a few items of interest. There's a page on spring flowers, and some information on roses. Also a section on growing fruit trees. I thought we might try one or two that I could use for preserves. Now put the book down and tell me what's new with the young girl's murder."

Hodgins put the book in his lap. "Very well, but I do believe you are becoming a little gruesome my Dear. I went to her burial this afternoon. Took Barnes with me. He seems particularly affected as he has a sister the same age. Noticed one of the neighbours acting oddly. When we got back to the station, there was a Captain from the New

York Police speaking with Draper."

He leaned forward and smiled. "You're going to like this bit. That second wife I was telling you about? Seems she's wanted in New York regarding the death of her husband."

Cordelia's eyes grew wide. "Oh that is a delicious bit of information. This is by far the most interesting case you've had for certain. Do you think she killed that poor child?"

Hodgins settled back. "Don't know what to think. Harrison, that's the Captain from New York, he doesn't think she would harm a child, but it's been several years since he knew her. We're going up to Pine Grove in the morning to get her. Right after arresting Nolan for having two wives that is. Will have to find out if she knew her husband was already married. It's gotten quite complicated." He closed his eyes and rested his head on the back of the chair.

"I wonder," Cordelia said.

He opened his eyes.

"Could she have found out that her husband was married and hired someone else to kill his daughter? That way she'd have him all to herself. He would be able to move up to Pine Grove and she would see him more."

He sat up. "Hire someone? Hmmm. Doubt there's

anyone in Pine Grove or the entire area that's a hired killer. Mostly farmers and merchants. But she does have a history in New York. Might know some undesirables down there. What made you think of it?"

"Why, I'm a woman. The only logical thing would be to dispose of any obstacles between me and my husband. Quite simple really."

Hodgins laughed. "Of course, quite logical. For a woman."

"Now, why don't you invite the Captain to dinner tomorrow? I'd like to meet a policeman from New York. He must have some interesting stories to tell."

CHAPTER 21

Hodgins arrived at the station to find Harrison already waiting.

"Early bird I see."

"Couldn't sleep. I'm anxious to finally catch up with Mary Cooper. Don't like to have cases left incomplete."

"As soon as Barnes arrives, we can go down to Nolan's. We'll have plenty of time to catch the first train afterwards. Shall we have a cup of tea? Barnes isn't due for a bit."

They chatted and reviewed their plans for the day. Barnes arrived about twenty minutes later and the three of them walked down to Duchess Street. There was a hired buggy out front and a trunk sitting on the porch. The front door was wide open. Hodgins knocked on the door frame and they walked in.

"Hello?"

"Be right down." The words floated from the second floor. Nolan came down the stairs carrying a satchel. He stopped mid-way when he saw Hodgins and Barnes.

"Do you have news?" He rushed the rest of the way down.

Nolan looked at Harrison but didn't ask who he was.

"Going somewhere?" Hodgins asked.

"Can't stay in this house. You understand."

"Where are you heading?"

"The farm in Pine Grove. You already know about that. Going to move there permanently."

"Yes. Did I tell you? I went back up there the other day. Met a very nice lady. Attractive too. A Mary Cooper. Or should I say Mary Nolan?"

Nolan dropped the satchel by his feet.

"Oh."

"Indeed. I'm placing you under arrest for bigamy. You do realize that you can't have more than one wife at a time?"

Nolan said nothing. Hodgins gestured to Barnes, who stepped forward with a set of handcuffs. Nolan put up no resistance.

"Constable Barnes will escort you back to the station while Captain Harrison and myself pay a visit to Miss Cooper. Oh, Captain Harrison is with the New York Police. Seems your lovely wife is wanted for murder. Did you know that?"

"No," Nolan whispered. "It's not possible." He

looked from Hodgins to Barnes. He started to sway. Barnes grabbed him.

"Olivia. Did she kill my daughter?"

"We don't know yet," Hodgins replied. "But we aim to find out."

* * *

Hodgins and Harrison got in the buggy Nolan had waiting and went to Union Station to take the first train to Woodbridge. They hired a buggy and went to Pine Grove to get Mary Cooper. They had decided that Harrison would stay in the buggy, hat pulled down, just in case she recognized him.

Hodgins knocked on the front door.

"Morning Detective. What brings ya up here a'gin?"

"I'm afraid there's been a bit of trouble. May I come in?"

She stepped back to let him enter and looked past him at Harrison. "What about yer friend?"

"We don't need him at the moment." He entered the house, closing the door behind him.

"We kin talk in here." She led him into the kitchen and plucked a cigar out of the jar sitting on the table. She lit it and leaned back in the chair. "So what's this all about?"

Hodgins was startled as he had never seen a woman smoke a cigar before. First the chewing tobacco and now this. *Interesting woman.* Ignoring his impulse to comment, he got on with the reason for his visit.

"I'm afraid your husband has been arrested."

"Arrested? Whatever for?"

Strange. She doesn't seem all that surprised.

"I don't know how to say this delicately, so I'll just say it in plain terms. When you married Kendall Nolan, he already had a wife."

He studied her face. There was no shock.

"Really?" She seemed calm.

She already knew.

"Had a daughter too. He's been arrested for bigamy."

"But if his wife is dead, then he's not a bigamist, is he?"

I never mentioned she was dead.

"She was quite alive when he married you."

"I see."

Hodgins watched as she processed the information.

"Oh, he wouldn't have . . ." Mary changed her mind and stopped. "What about the girl? I ain't taking care of his kin."

Hodgins thought she seemed to be rather cold and unfeeling.

"She was murdered."

The stunned look on her face revealed she hadn't

known.

"Who wouldn't have done what, Mary? What were you going to say?"

"Nothing. When did she get herself killed?"

"Almost two weeks ago."

"So that's why he's bin so funny lately."

Hodgins continued with the script he and Harrison had worked out. He was certain that she had not killed the girl or hired someone else to do it.

"I'd like you to come back to Toronto with me. Confirm Mr. Nolan is the man you married."

"I'd like ta come to the city. Nothin' much to do out here."

He pulled out his pocket watch.

"We need to leave if we're to catch the next train back."

After she was settled in the buggy beside Harrison, he raised his head and pushed his hat back.

"Hello Mary. Been keeping well?"

It only took a minute for her to figure out who he was. She swore and tried to get off the buggy, but Hodgins was blocking her way. She was pinned in between them.

"What's the matter?" Hodgins asked. "Aren't you happy to see an old friend? Don't you want to see your husband?"

She crossed her arms over her chest and stared straight ahead. She didn't speak another word all the way to Toronto.

* * *

When they arrived back at the station, Mary was put in the interrogation room, alone. Hodgins and Harrison sat at Hodgins' desk. Now that Mary was out of sight they could speak freely. Hodgins filled Harrison in on the conversation in Mary's kitchen.

"She already knew Nolan was married. I'm certain of that. But it was a surprise that his daughter was dead. She started to say something but stopped. I wonder if maybe she knows who might have done it."

"What exactly did she say?"

"Let me think. Something like *he wouldn't* or *couldn't*, then stopped. Wouldn't elaborate on that. Maybe now we've got her here she'll say more."

"Do you know if there's a hired hand at the farm?"

"Don't know. Why?"

"Saw a man out back while you were inside. When he saw me looking at him he ducked behind the house. Didn't get a good look, but he seemed familiar. I think he was maybe in his thirties, but he was too far away to be certain."

"If he worked there he'd have no reason to hide.

Could be that's who she was referring to. When I glanced out the kitchen window I saw someone go into the barn." Hodgins stood.

"Shall we get started?" He asked.

Captain Harrison nodded and followed Hodgins into the interrogation room. Mary sat at the far end of a long table, hands folded and resting on her lap. She didn't acknowledge either man. Hodgins and Harrison sat on opposite sides, surrounding her as they had done on the trip into Toronto.

"Mary, you know you'll be taken back to New York with Captain Harrison and stand trial for the murder of your husband. It might be helpful if you told us what you know about the murder of Olivia Nolan. It will show you are cooperative. If the jurors find out you were involved with the death of a young girl, they won't show you any mercy."

Mary stared at the wall and continued her vigilance of silence.

Harrison stood up and shoved his face in front of her. "Damn it woman. Say something."

He grabbed her hands and slammed them on the table top. She winced.

"Hold on there Harrison. No need to be so rough." Hodgins grabbed Harrison by the wrist. "I don't go in for that sort of thing. Leastways not with a woman, cold as she might be."

Harrison released his grip but did not back away from her.

"Maybe if we let her sit in a cell she'll feel more like talking," Hodgins said. "We've got Nolan down there and he knows all about her. Even thinks she killed his daughter. Might prove interesting to have them side by side. If Nolan doesn't get to her, maybe the rats will. They're quite large you know."

Hodgins took Mary's arm. She pulled away and stood up. They escorted her down to the cells and locked her in next to Nolan. He rushed over and reached through the bars.

"Come here you bitch. I'll get you for what you did to Olivia."

Mary backed away. "No, it weren't me."

"I hate you for what you've done."

Mary ran to the front of the cell, grabbing the bars with both hands. "You have to let me out. Lock me up if ya must, but not here."

Nolan was still reaching through the bars, trying to grab hold of her. "You murdering bitch. I'll kill you for what you've done."

Nolan sank to the floor sobbing. "My precious

Olivia."

Hodgins turned to Harrison. "We don't get many woman in our cells, but they generally will do anything to get out. Nolan seems convinced she did it. Between the rats and Nolan, she's certain to break down. Guess she's surrounded by rats." Hodgins laughed at his joke.

Harrison grumbled about not having more time with her, but did as Hodgins wanted. They left her to the barrage of insults and threats coming from Nolan.

Since they had been in such a rush to get Mary Cooper into a jail cell, lunch had been forgotten until their stomachs rumbled. They went out and got a meat pie from one of the street vendors.

"Have you been to Toronto before, Captain?"

"No, first trip. Thought it might be much like New York, but it's not. Not so crowded. Seems a bit more peaceful. Rather enjoy the bustle of the city myself."

"I guess it's all what you're used to. It's not always quiet though. Especially down by the waterfront. Had our fair share of riots too, mostly courtesy of the Orangemen. Even had a circus riot back in '55 that involved the Orangemen. Clowns, if you can imagine. Because of a brothel."

Harrison looked skeptical. "Clowns and a brothel? You're pulling my leg."

159

"No, not at all. It really happened."

The both had a good laugh and shared a few off colour jokes over that.

"Any more thoughts about the man you saw at the farm? If he seemed familiar, maybe he's an old acquaintance of Mary's?"

"I'm sure I should know him, but it's been five years since I dealt with her," Harrison said. "Will have to remember who she associated with back then. It'll come to me eventually."

"Before I forget, my wife has insisted you join us for supper tonight."

CHAPTER 22

Cordelia rushed around getting everything ready. She was able to find enough flowers between the weeds to make a nice centrepiece for the table. Sara had been given her supper early and was told to stay upstairs out of the grown-ups way. She whined enough that she was allowed to meet Captain Harrison *then* she had to go straight upstairs.

At six thirty a knock sounded on the door. Sara held onto Scraps while Hodgins answered it.

"Good of you to join us. Come in. Excuse the disarray but we've just moved in and are still putting the house in order."

Scraps barked.

"Nice dog ya got there," Harrison said.

The dog pulled away from Sara and bounded down the hall towards Harrison, tail wagging excitedly. Hodgins grabbed him before he could jump up.

"He gets rather excitable when new people come by."

Harrison stroked the top of the dog's head, and

Scraps' tail thumped against the floor. Cordelia came out of the kitchen and stood with Sara.

"I'd like you to meet my family. My wife, Cordelia, and our daughter, Sara. You've already met Scraps."

Harrison walked over to Cordelia and handed her a box of chocolates. He reached into his pocket and pulled out a bag of sweets for Sara.

"Thank you for inviting me."

Sara was sent upstairs for the evening and Hodgins and Harrison went into the sitting room. Scraps followed. Cordelia went back to the kitchen to finish preparing their meal. She had picked up a nice piece of roasting beef, potatoes, carrots, and onions. The roast was sitting in it's drippings, soaking up the flavour.

Hodgins had purchased a bottle of wine for the occasion. That was one thing that was missing from the house as spirits were not at the top of the shopping list. Too many necessities to purchase first. His father-in-law always had whiskey on hand, but it wasn't something Hodgins had a great love for.

The wine was sat breathing on the dining room table. Hodgins wasn't really certain what that meant, but his wife said it was necessary.

Cordelia placed the beef on a platter and the vegetables in bowls. One by one she took them to the table. She frowned as she surveyed the settings. They didn't have anything they could consider their best dishes. Not yet anyway. At least it was a full set of dishes and there were no cracks or chips. Satisfied that everything was presentable, she called the men into the dining room and they made small talk over their meal.

When Cordelia served the cake she had made earlier in the day, she asked about Olivia's murder. Harrison looked at Hodgins and raised an eyebrow.

"Not to worry. My wife seems to enjoy discussing my cases. Very special woman, my Cordelia."

"Special indeed." Harrison wasn't sure what he should say. "Go into much detail?"

"Well, some. Depends on the circumstances. Didn't go into all the details about this one, what with it being so brutal, and a young girl."

"I'm a strong woman Captain Harrison, but I do have a daughter. I didn't want to hear exactly how she died. My husband generally knows when to stop. So, have you learned anything new?"

"Still mulling over your suggestion that Miss Cooper, the second wife, hired someone to kill the girl. So far there's nothing pointing in that direction. Not ruling it out though."

Harrison looked across the table at Cordelia. "You

suggested that? Whatever made you come up with that conclusion?"

"Woman's logic," Hodgins said. He grinned.

"It's quite simple really." She explained it to Harrison much the same way she told her husband. "Women will often take drastic measures to get or keep a man."

Both men laughed. Cordelia stood up. "I really don't see why that is so funny." She picked up the empty plates and stormed into the kitchen.

"I think we've offended your good wife."

"She'll calm down quick enough. Delia really does come up with some very insightful thoughts. Don't mind admitting she's helped me more than once."

"Glad to hear you acknowledging it." Cordelia said, coming out of the kitchen with a fresh pot of tea. "Now, tell me about Mrs. Nolan, or Miss Cooper, or whatever you're calling her. What did you find out from her?"

"She's not sayin' much," Harrison said. "Knows she's going to be facing a murder trial back in New York. Should've seen her when we threw her in the cell beside Nolan. If there wasn't bars between them, your husband would have another murder on his hands."

"Goodness! Whatever happened?"

"Nolan's sure she killed his daughter," Hodgins said. "I won't repeat some of the things he called her."

Cordelia blushed slightly. "I think I can imagine."

"She knows something though," Hodgins said. "She started to say something to me back at the farm but changed her mind. She seemed genuinely shocked when I mentioned the murder of the girl."

"Don't forget about that man I saw hiding behind the farm house," Harrison said. "Wish I got a better look at 'im. Still can't place him."

"Farm hand?" Cordelia asked. She turned to her husband. "Was it a working farm?"

Hodgins shrugged. "Why hide if he was a hired hand?"

Cordelia nodded in agreement. "So, maybe he was a hired hand, just not for the farm. Someone she knew from New York possibly?"

"Back to that again?" Hodgins smiled and turned to Harrison. "If she wasn't a woman she would make a good detective."

Harrison almost choked on his tea. "A woman detective?" he said when he finished coughing. "Never happen. Can you imagine? Suppose you also think woman will be running the country some day too. Preposterous."

Cordelia sat back and crossed her arms. "And why not? Not all women are mindless and feeble. Just like not all men are smart and strong."

"Bah," Harrison said. "Never happen."

"Let's not get into politics, please," Hodgins said. "Murder's much more interesting and less volatile, so to speak."

"So what are you going to do tomorrow? Beat a confession out of her?"

"Cordelia," Hodgins exclaimed. "I do not beat my prisoners, often. And never a woman."

She smiled.

"You're husband's a little too protective if you ask me. She's a murderer first, woman second. Maybe you should move her *into* Nolan's cell. Just for a few minutes."

"What you do with your prisoners in New York is your concern. Until you take her, she's my concern." Hodgins thought about what might happen if the two were put together, then smiled briefly.

"Might be interesting though. Putting them in the same cell I mean."

They talked a bit longer, then Cordelia cleared up while Hodgins and Harrison went back to the sitting room. They drank wine, argued good naturedly over the treatment of prisoners and laughed some more about women running the country before Harrison went back to his hotel for the night.

CHAPTER 23

Harrison came up to the station mid-morning and sat with Hodgins in the interrogation room. Mary Cooper was brought in. She didn't seem quite as defiant after spending the night in the dank cell with the rats and an angry husband for a neighbour. Hodgins had been told that sometime during the night Nolan threw his full bedpan at the bars separating the two cells.

Mary was deflated, withdrawn. She sat in the chair at the end of the table, just as she had the day before. Again, she stared at the wall. This time she slumped a little. The hardness had left her face. Hodgins got up and went to the far side of the room, indicating for Harrison to follow.

Hodgins spoke quietly. "I think she may talk now. The night in the cell seems to have taken all the fight out of her. Nolan's reaction to her probably put her over the top."

Harrison looked over at Mary. "You're right. She seems much more placated. Maybe too much so. Looks to me like she's gone inside herself, if you know what I mean.

Then again, it might all be an act."

"Guess we'll find out soon enough. I think gentle methods are required."

Harrison snorted. "Gentle methods. Not in my jail."

"It's not your jail."

They took their places at the table. Hodgins touched her arm.

"Mary."

She slowly turned her head and looked at him. He removed his hand.

"Mary, what do you know about Olivia's death?"

"Nothing." Her voice was barely audible.

"How did you know that Nolan was already married? When did you find out?"

"Few weeks ago." She sighed. "Might as well tell you." She looked over at Harrison. "I'm gonna hang anyway."

Harrison slammed his palm on the table. Mary jumped. "I knew she killed her husband five years ago. As good as just admitted it."

"I'm not concerned about that. Mary, how did you find out Nolan was married?"

Mary glanced sideways at Harrison. "Freddie Calhoon."

"Four Fingers Freddie? How the hell would he know that?" Harrison asked. "Wait a minute. Is that who was hiding out at the farm?"

"Four Fingers Freddie?" Hodgins said. "Should I even ask?"

"Lost the thumb off his left hand in a knife fight. Made him even more ornery than he was to start with. Mary used to keep company with him. We thought he might've been the one who done in her husband, but he was playing cards and drinking when the man was poisoned. Not his style anyway. Quite handy with a knife, except that one time."

"So, this Four Fingers Freddie is in Toronto?" Hodgins asked Mary.

"Yes. I sent him a letter. Asked him to come up and follow Kendall. He was away so much, just didn't seem right. Sent Freddie the train fare and he came right away."

Mary stopped talking and stared blankly at the wall again.

"Mary," Hodgins said. He touched her arm again. "Mary." No response. He turned to Harrison. "I don't think she's going to say anything more right now."

Mary was put back in her cell and the men headed towards Hodgins' office. Harrison glanced out the window and stopped. "There."

"What?" Hodgins said.

"That man over there. I'm sure that's Calhoon."

Hodgins looked out the window as Harrison ran out the front door and across the street.

"Shit."

Hodgins ran after him. The man ran down Regent Street, Harrison close behind. Calhoon was getting away.

Should have called him Fast Freddie, Hodgins thought as he caught up to Harrison. They ran past St. David Street and saw Calhoon turn left on Sydenham, then left again at Sackville. Hodgins could see Freddie had stopped at Queen and was looking both ways repeatedly, trying to figure out where to go. He turned around. Hodgins and Harrison gained ground.

"We've got 'im now," Harrison said.

Calhoon turned left on Queen, then scurried down St. Paul's. Harrison stopped to catch his breath. "Damn. Bugger's getting' away."

"Maybe not. That's a dead end street he just turned down. Don't recall if there are any fences though. We might still catch him."

As they approached St. Paul's Street, Calhoon was just exiting back onto Queen. He quickly turned around and went back down. The street ended at the back of a large building. There appeared to be no exit. Calhoon turned and pulled a knife.

"Get back or I'll run ya clear through."

"There's one of him and two of us. We can rush him," Hodgins suggested.

"Last time I had him in my jail, it took five of my men to subdue him. Two ended up in the hospital."

"Great. Any suggestions? Is he wanted?"

"Always have my eye on him, but he's not wanted right now."

Hodgins thought for a moment. "Maybe we can talk to him. If he's not wanted, he's got nothing to be afraid of."

"Ha. Not Freddie. He's not a talker. And he hates all cops."

Hodgins took a few steps toward Calhoon.

"I ain't kiddin'. Come any closer and them'll be yer last steps."

Calhoon made stabbing motions with the knife. Hodgins took a few more steps.

"Either yer mighty brave or awful foolish," Harrison said. He took a step forward.

Hodgins noticed movement at the end of the lane. He moved back with Harrison and spoke softly. "Look at the back of the road."

"Where the hell did he come from?"

At the very back, creeping around some crates, was Constable Barnes. His arm hit a crate and it toppled over.

Calhoon turned.

Hodgins ran forward. Barnes approached cautiously. Harrison swore and ran to help.

Calhoon turned back and forth between Hodgins and Barnes, swinging the knife. Every time Calhoon turned towards Barnes, Hodgins took another step closer. Harrison circled around. Hodgins was just beyond the reach of the knife. Calhoon turned towards Barnes again, and Hodgins tackled him.

They hit the ground. Harrison tried to help, but they were rolling so much he couldn't get a grip on Calhoon. Barnes ran up, holding a piece of broken crate.

Calhoon and Hodgins stopped rolling, with Calhoon on the top. Barnes slammed the wood down on Calhoon's back. He fell to the side and Hodgins sat up. Calhoon staggered to his feet and Harrison leveled him with a punch to the jaw. Calhoon fell back, unconscious.

"Where did you come from Henry?" Hodgins asked Barnes.

"I noticed the Captain here rush out, then you, so I followed. When I saw the man run down St. Paul's I went down Sackville. There's several small alleyways, like that one over there." He pointed to the alley between Queen Street and where the scuffle had taken place. "There's another one right at the end of the lane, just before the last

172

building."

"Calhoon must not have gone right to the end before turning back," Hodgins said. "Let's get him back to the station." He started to stand and fell back, gripping his side.

"Sir? Are you all right?" Barnes asked.

Hodgins pulled his hand away. His palm was red. "Seems I may have gotten in the way of his knife."

CHAPTER 24

Barnes and Harrison half carried, half dragged Calhoon up to the station house. Hodgins trailed behind holding his side. Harrison took Calhoon inside and got him locked up while Barnes assisted Hodgins up to the hospital on Gerrard.

The wound wasn't deep and Hodgins refused to stay in the hospital. He was stitched and bandaged and went back to the station house.

"Has our friend come to yet?" he asked Harrison.

"Yeah, a little while ago. Your jails getting' mighty full. He wants to know what he's being charged with. Told him we hadn't been planning to arrest him, least ways not until he assaulted a fellow officer. You're more than welcome to have him." Harrison laughed. "Keep him off my streets for awhile. Guess your cut ain't too bad or they wouldn't a let ya out."

"Doctor said I was lucky. If it hadda gone any deeper it would have cut into my kidney." Hodgins winced as he lowered himself into the chair behind his desk.

"I think you should go home," Barnes said. "Rest up a bit."

"Nonsense. As long as I don't get into another barney I'll be fine. I think we'll let Calhoon stew in the cell for a while before questioning him. Is there still an officer down by the cells? If Mary gets too close to Nolan, he'll probably strangle her through the bars."

"Yes, Riley's down there."

"Good. Have a word with him. Tell him to keep an ear out for any conversation between Calhoon and Mary."

Barnes nodded and went to talk to Riley.

Hodgins was getting hungry so he opened the lunch Cordelia had packed. Leftovers from last evenings meal. She had put in extra for Harrison. Hodgins went to the back for tea, then spread the beef, bread, and cake across his desk.

As Barnes walked past the office, he noticed the constable eyeing the cake and licking his lips. Cordelia had packed an overly generous slab, so Hodgins broke off a piece of the cake, waved Barnes in, and handed it to him.

"Thank you, Sir. I do so like your wife's chocolate cake." He stuffed it in his mouth as he continued to his desk. Hodgins could hear the sounds of pleasure as Barnes chewed.

"That boy certainly does enjoy his food," Hodgins said

to Harrison. "Especially sweets."

Hodgins felt a little better after he filled his belly; almost made his side hurt less.

"Have to make sure that the dog is under control before entering the house tonight." He put his hand to his side. "Today's not a good day to have a large, over-friendly dog," he said to Harrison.

Hodgins grasped the arms of his chair and made to stand up. A sharp pain ripped through his side and he lowered himself back down. He took a deep breath and tried again, slowly this time.

"Shall we take a stab at getting Calhoon to talk?" He placed his hand on his side. "Bad choice of words."

"You're a stubborn man, Detective," Harrison said.

Hodgins ignored the comment and waved Barnes over.

"Bring Calhoon up to the interrogation room. Check with Riley to see if Cooper or Nolan said anything useful. They may have argued and forgot there was a copper listening. He waited with Harrison in the interrogation room for Calhoon to arrive. Barnes entered behind Calhoon and shook his head, indicating Riley heard nothing. He took out the key to the handcuffs, but Harrison stopped him.

"I don't think that's wise boy. Leave him cuffed."

Barnes looked over at Hodgins.

"Leave him."

Barnes left, but stayed outside the door.

"I guess you know Captain Harrison. Why did you run off?" Hodgins asked.

"He's a copper. Don't need no other reason."

"What brings you up to our fair city?"

"Holiday?" Calhoon suggested.

"That's not what Miss Cooper said."

Hodgins looked at Harrison and nodded. They had already agreed to let Harrison take the lead. Hodgins didn't have the strength to deal with someone like Calhoon and he didn't want him to find out he had been stabbed.

Harrison had Calhoon's knife. He got up and stood beside him.

"Nice blade." How'd ya like to find out how it feels?"

He held the blade against Calhoon's neck, just hard enough for his skin to indent. Calhoon didn't flinch.

"We know Mary had you come up to spy on her so-called husband. What else did you do?"

He moved the knife so the tip pressed into Calhoon's neck, then pushed until a thin trickle of blood appeared. Harrison looked over at Hodgins.

"Try not to mess up the floor. Blood's a bugger to clean up." Hodgins was torn between stopping Harrison and letting him continue but the pain in his side won, for now anyhow.

Calhoon remained still. He shifted his eyes to look at Hodgins.

"It ain't a crime to watch somebody."

"No," Hodgins said, "but you did assault a police officer."

Calhoon moved and a bit more blood trickled out. "You started it. You jumped me. I should charge you."

Hodgins shrugged. "Who's the judge going to believe?"

"What do ya want to know?" Calhoon growled.

"Miss Cooper. What did she have you come up for?"

"Like Mary told ya. To follow that Nolan guy."

Harrison pressed harder on the knife.

Calhoon sat still, not wanting to draw more blood. His lips barely moved.

"I told ya what you wanted to know. She didn't ask me to do nothin' else."

Hodgins looked over at the window and waved Barnes into the room. "Take him back to his cell."

Barnes walked over to Calhoon but Harrison still had the knife to his throat.

"Captain," Hodgins said. "That's enough."

Harrison hesitated before removing the knife. After

Barnes had taken Calhoon away Harrison turned to Hodgins.

"I coulda got him to talk. Just needed a bit more coaxing is all."

"Not today." Hodgins placed both hands on the table and rose slowly.

"I think I'll take Barnes' advice and go home after all. You're welcome to stay and go over everything with Barnes. Nothing more."

Harrison grumbled and nodded in agreement. Hodgins spoke to Barnes, leaving explicit instructions not to allow Harrison access to their three prisoners. He also asked him to go see Dr. McKenzie and find out everything he could about Mrs. Nolan's death last year. He then took a very rough, very bumpy, and very painful carriage ride home.

CHAPTER 25

After spending the previous evening being pampered by his family, Hodgins was ready to return to work. He hated lying around the house, and he didn't feel his injury was that bad. Cordelia tried to get him to stay home for a few more days, but he wouldn't listen.

"That Webster fellow should be in town today. I need to track him down before he disappears again."

"Surely Constable Barnes and Captain Harrison can speak to him."

"No. Don't want Harrison talking to him alone. Barnes is only a constable, and still new. Harrison will run roughshod over him. Don't want him scaring off Webster. He can be quite the bully." He hadn't told Cordelia about Harrison drawing blood from Calhoon.

He kissed Cordelia and headed out. The walk took twice as long as usual but he wasn't up for any more jostling on a buggy or trolley. Harrison had arrived before him and was with Barnes. It sounded as though he was taking over. Barnes looked relieved to see Hodgins.

Harrison turned to face the detective

"How much longer are you going to hold Mary Cooper? Seems to me the only thing she's done wrong was marrying Nolan. No law against being stupid, leastways not in New York. I'd like to take her back for trial."

"Once I'm certain whether or not she was involved in the girl's death, then you can have her. 'Course even if she was involved, I suppose you'll have to take her anyway. You were looking for her first. Send her back if you find she's innocent. If she's not, well, can't have a trial for a corpse, and can't hang her twice. End of the week suit you?"

"Bin waiting this long, another couple days won't make no never mind."

"Detective Hodgins," the desk sergeant called.

Hodgins turned and the sergeant waved him over. "Man here to see you. Got one of your cards."

He walked over and the young man held his hand out. "My name's John Webster. My folks said you wanted to see me. Something about Olivia Nolan? Tragic what happened. Not sure why you want to see me though."

"Come into to my office."

Hodgins perched on the front edge of the desk and Webster took the chair. He studied Webster's appearance. It was easy to see why women fell for him: Good looking young man; bit of a twinkle in his eyes; long dark wavy hair, just past his shoulders. *Dark and wavy? Just like the one found on Olivia.*

"Did you see or hear anything that night? Someone creeping around? Anyone around during the day who looked suspicious?"

"No, no one that I can recall. I've been here often enough to know all the neighbours. Didn't see anyone who didn't belong."

"What was your relationship with Miss Nolan? I understand you were," he paused. "Friendly?"

Webster looked down at the floor and whispered, "We were to be married." There was a slight tremble in his voice.

"That's not what I've heard. Didn't she turn you down? More than once?"

Webster's head snapped up. "Yes, but only because she thought it too soon, that she was too young. We would have married when she was a little older."

Hodgins looked through his notebook. "Understand you had a bit of bother with your former employer. A Mr. Adams? Something to do with his daughter."

Webster's ears turned red. "That was over a year ago."

"I see. And your current employer, Mr. Purdy, seems to think he needs to keep you away from his daughter. If you were planning to marry Miss Nolan, why carry on with another?"

Webster smiled. "I'm a young man. Not married *yet*."

"Miss Nolan's friends told me that she wanted nothing to do with you. That you were bothering her. Are you certain you didn't see her that night? Tried something on, and killed her when she said no?"

Webster stood, clenching his fists. "How dare you? I would never hurt Olivia. Never."

"Calm down. I need to eliminate people. You do want to find out who did it, don't you? Where were you that night?"

Webster remained standing for a moment, then slowly sunk back into the chair. "I suppose you're just doing your job. I was at the boarding house with Miss O'Hara."

"Until what time?"

Webster said nothing.

"You're not suggesting you were with her all night, are you?"

Webster smiled. "No, all's the pity. She's quite a handsome woman. I did convince her not to go across to the Nolan house, but alas that's *all* I could convince her of."

"Right. I'll confirm that with Miss O'Hara." Hodgins called Barnes over. He stood and whispered so Webster couldn't hear.

"Did you look into the death of that painter fellow? Was he married?"

"Yes, I mean no. Yes, I spoke to Constable Smith. No the painter wasn't married. Recluse actually."

"So there's no reason to believe the two murders were connected. No love triangle involving Webster?"

"No, doesn't seem so."

"Blast."

Hodgins dismissed Barnes and turned back to Webster.

"That's all for now. But you're not to leave town until I say so."

"But I have my calls to make. People are expecting me. I'll lose orders."

"Hang your orders. I'm trying to find out who killed your *fiancé*. Until I'm convinced you had nothing to do with it, you will stay put."

"But –"

"I suggest you send word to your customers."

Hodgins remained standing. Webster took the hint and left, then Hodgins went over to Barnes' desk to speak with Barnes and Harrison.

"What have you found out about Mrs. Nolan's death?"

"Nothin' useful,' Harrison said. "She was sick for some time. Nothin' suspicious according to your doctor."

"Sir," Barnes said. "I recalled you mentioned that woman what disappeared over on George Street. I asked around about that."

"And?"

"Turns out she'd run off with her boyfriend. Her friend received a postcard from her the other day. Seems they just got on the train and went to Alberta."

"So it's just a coincidence we have two murders and a disappearance in the same neighbourhood about the same time . . . Damn."

He sat on the desk beside Barnes. "Let's think this through. We have three suspects. Four maybe. Mr. Nolan, Miss Cooper, and Mr. Webster. Not really convinced about Cooper and Nolan. It's just a feeling. I have no evidence one way or the other. They're not at the top of the list, but I'm keeping an open mind about them. What about Calhoon?" He turned to Harrison.

"Could Calhoon harm a young girl?"

"Hmmm. He's quite ruthless, but a young girl? I've seen him slap around the boys who do jobs for him, but he actually seems to have a soft spot for the ladies."

"What about Olivia's father?" Hodgins asked. "He's genuinely grief-stricken. Then again, it could be guilt. With her out of the picture, he could move in with Miss Cooper and keep up the pretense of being legitimately married. He was in the process of doing just that when we arrested him. 'Course he's not too fond of her now."

Harrison joined in. "Mary Cooper is already under suspicion for murdering her husband, and I truly believe she's got it in her. You may not think so, but I'm certain she'll be convicted for that one."

"What about Mr. Webster?" Barnes asked. "We know he's a rogue, but a murderer?"

"Crime of passion maybe?" Hodgins said. "We have four suspects. We need to narrow it down. Get me some paper, will you Henry?"

Barnes pulled a pad of long paper from his desk drawer and handed it to Hodgins.

The detective got off the desk and took a deep breath as a pain shot through his side. He put the pad down and spoke as he wrote.

"Nolan said he was out of town. The stationmaster or one of the porters can confirm that. I have the name of the customer he claims he had business with. Barnes, you take care of checking that. If he has two witnesses to say he was out of town, then we can cross him off.

Webster said he was with Miss O'Hara. I'll speak to her and find out what time that was. 'Course he could've snuck out afterwards, so he can't be completely eliminated.

Hodgins turned to Harrison. "Since you're familiar with Calhoon, would you like to have another go at him? *Without* the knife this time?"

Harrison made a fist and smacked it against his other palm. "Let me at 'im. I'll find out anything ya need to know."

"Just make sure he's still breathing when I return."

CHAPTER 26

Hodgins left to go down to Miss O'Hara's wondering what shape Calhoon would be in when he returned. What should have been a pleasant fifteen minute walk took painfully closer to thirty, but he wasn't going to let his wound stop him from doing his job.

He leaned heavily on the railing as he dragged his aching body up onto the large verandah of the boarding house. He paused to catch his breath before knocking on the front door.

"Good morning Miss O'Hara. I need to ask you a few more questions."

"Certainly Detective." Flossie joined him outside. "Shall we sit? It's nice and shady." She pointed to the white wicker chairs arranged around a small table at the east end of the porch.

Hodgins waited until she was seated before gingerly lowering himself onto the chair. He pulled out his notebook and pencil.

"Mr. Webster said that he was here with you the evening that Miss Nolan was killed. Is that true?"

"Oh, I'm so ashamed for what I did. If I hadn't let Mr. Webster talk me out of staying with Olivia she'd still be alive."

"Or you might very well be dead too," Hodgins mumbled. Unfortunately he spoke louder than he intended.

Flossie's mouth opened and she gasped. Hodgins thought she looked pale and feared she might faint.

"I do apologize. I should never have suggested such a thing." He waited until her colour returned.

"How late were you with him?"

"We played cards with my other lodger and my friend, Cecelia Groves, until about ten, then we sat and talked until close to midnight. They went up to their rooms, Cecelia went home, and I checked to make sure all the doors were locked before I retired."

"And he didn't leave after that?"

"No, I don't believe so. Leastways I didn't hear him. There's a squeaky step on the staircase and my room is closest to the top. The house remained quiet. I'm certain I would have heard if anyone went downstairs."

"Has anyone stayed in the room Mr. Webster rented?"

"No, since he's here regularly, I keep the room vacant

for him. I'm rarely filled up, unfortunately."

Hodgins wrote down what she told him then put away his notebook. He stood slowly.

"Would you mind if I had a look in his room? He knew Miss Nolan and there might be something useful tucked away."

"Certainly. It's this way." She rose and Hodgins followed her up to the second floor. The third step from the top squeaked loudly as she stepped on it.

"See. I told you I would've heard if someone went out after retiring. It's quite loud now and seems so much louder at night."

She walked down the hall and stopped at the last door. Hodgins was experimenting, putting his weight down at different spots. The step squeaked each time.

"I suppose someone could hop over that one, but I guess he wouldn't land quietly." He went down to the door that Miss O'Hara had opened.

"I've cleaned the room and I assure you he left nothing behind."

Hodgins entered the room, quickly surveying it. He walked over to the dresser and opened the drawers, one by one. Each was empty. There was one shelf on the wall, and a small table sat beside the bed. Both were empty.

"If you do come across something of his, anything at

all, please contact me right away. I won't keep you any longer. Thank you for your time."

Thirty minutes later he was back at the station house. Barnes was at his desk, but Harrison was no where to be seen.

"Where is he then?" he asked Barnes.

"Still with Calhoon." Barnes looked uncomfortable. "He told me to leave. There was a lot of noise, but it's been quiet for some time now."

"Damn. You should *never* have left him alone with Calhoon."

"But he's a Captain, Sir."

"A Captain *and* a bully. Not your fault. Come with me."

They hurried to the interrogation room. Hodgins grimaced and held his side. He glanced through the window as he passed.

"What the . . . "

"Hodgins opened the door. "Get out. Out of this room and out of my station."

"Oh dear Lord," Barnes said, peering around Hodgins.

Calhoon was sitting against the wall, Harrison kneeling in front, fist raised for another strike. Calhoon's face was a bloody, pulpy mess. Blood dripped from Harrison's knuckles.

"Get some of the boys," Hodgins said to Barnes. "We need to get him up to the hospital, if it's not already too late."

Barnes ran for help. Harrison had not moved. Hodgins stormed over, grabbed Harrison' raised arm and yanked him to his feet, ignoring the searing pain in his side.

"I said *get out*. I don't want to see your face in this station again. I'll have Miss Cooper brought over to your hotel when we're finished with her. Better yet, why don't you just go back to New York on the next train, and I'll have her escorted down."

Hodgins pushed Harrison out of the room as Barnes rushed down the hall with two other constables.

Harrison sneered, "You're all too soft. He was ready to talk. Just needed a bit more coaxing."

"A bit more of your coaxing and I'd be calling the coroner. For your sake he'd better recover. Go back to the hotel, now." Hodgins kept pushing Harrison until he stumbled out the front door.

The two constables came out carrying Calhoon, one on either side of him. It looked like they were supporting a drunk. Barnes followed. Hodgins reached for Barnes.

"Stay here, they can manage. It's only a couple of blocks."

"Sir, I think you should accompany them up to the hospital." He pointed to the front of Hodgins shirt. A small red spot had appeared and was slowly expanding.

Hodgins looked down. "Must have loosened a stitch. Nothing to worry about."

They stood on the steps; Hodgins glaring at Harrison's back while Barnes watched the constables carry Calhoon around the corner and out of sight.

"I told Smith to stay at the hospital and bring back word soon as the doctors are finished. Hope that's all right?"

"Good thinking. I don't trust Harrison. Wouldn't put it past him to double back and have a go at Calhoon in the hospital. Might put him off to see the police there. If Smith isn't back in a few hours, I'll go up and check on him. Have one of the lads stay overnight if need be."

They went back inside and over to Barnes' desk. Hodgins picked up the paper he had been writing on earlier and re-read the names.

"I'm sure Nolan didn't kill his daughter. Don't know if he would've hired someone. Who knows what type of characters he meets on his travels. Still need to confirm where he was."

"I've sent a telegram to his customer in Coboconk. I'll go to the train station and see if anyone remembers seeing him that day."

"I'm also certain Miss Cooper didn't do it. Unless she's a very good actress, I believe she was unaware the girl was killed. That leaves Webster and Calhoon. Unless it was totally random, then we're back to the beginning. I have a feeling it was deliberate though. Whoever did it must have known she was alone in the house. Don't know how Calhoon would know that, but Webster made certain Miss O'Hara stayed away from the Nolan house."

"But why would Webster kill her? He said he wanted to marry her."

"My wife probably has some logical theory on that," Hodgins mumbled.

"Sir?"

"Nothing. Miss O'Hara seems quite certain no one left the boarding house after she locked up though. The step has quite a distinctive and loud squeak. I suppose if someone wanted to, they could've avoided that particular step somehow. Don't forget to go to the station and see if anyone remembers seeing Nolan that day. I think I'll have another chat with Miss Cooper. I have a feeling there's something she's not telling me."

* * *

Since the interrogation room still had blood splattered about, and Chief Draper was out for the rest of the day,

Hodgins had Miss Cooper brought to Draper's office as it was more private than his. She was even more withdrawn than before.

"Miss Cooper. Mary. Is there anything else you can tell me? Did you ask Calhoon to come up for any reason other than to watch Nolan?"

She sat with her hands in her lap and seemed focused on the edge of the desk. She said nothing.

"What happened when Calhoon told you about Olivia?"

She raised her head and looked directly at him. "Happened?"

"Yes, when you found out that your husband had been married for years and had a daughter, what did you do? You must've been angry."

"I was shocked, but when Freddie told me Kendall's wife was dead, figured it didn't much matter now. Except for that girl. I wanted my husband home more, but he couldn't stay because of her."

"So you wished her harm? Wanted her out of the way?"

She looked shocked. "Freddie suggested the same thing, but it wasn't her fault. Damn girl was a hindrance. Not worth killing though."

"You never asked him to get rid of Olivia then?"

"No, only to follow Kendall and find out why he was away so much. I ain't all that educated, but I know salesmen don't spend that much time away from home. I knew somethin' was up."

"How did you meet Nolan?"

She smiled. "On the train. We got to chatting and he invited me to lunch. I had just moved up from New York and didn't know a soul. He spent money on me and I liked it. I think he was trying to re-live his youth. At first he was just someone to buy me things, but he kinda grew on me. When he proposed, I said yes." She shrugged

"Knowing what I do now, I guess his wife was sickly and he was in need of female companionship, if ya know what I mean. Never understood why he insisted we live in the country. Suppose he didn't want me bumping into any of his friends."

Hodgins watched her closely as she answered his questions.

When she was first brought up from the cell she kept her eyes down, refusing to acknowledge him. As soon as he suggested she had something to do with Olivia's murder, she changed. Her head snapped up. Was more alert, but not too defensive. She responded the way people generally do when accused of something they didn't do.

Over the years, Hodgins had developed a sense for

when people were hiding something. He decided she was innocent. At least of this. She had never denied killing her husband five years earlier when it was mentioned, and he didn't feel the need to bring it up again.

"I'll be sending you back to New York with Harrison tomorrow. I'd wish you luck, but I think we both know how that's going to turn out."

She smiled weakly. "I've had a good life so far. Well, maybe not good, but definitely fun."

He signalled the constable who had been standing guard, to come in.

"Take her back to her cell. First thing tomorrow take her to Harrison at his hotel. He'll be taking custody of her. Escort them both to the train and see them off."

Hodgins remained in Draper's office, thinking. Calhoon seemed more than agreeable to help Mary. She couldn't have much money to pay him to come up. She'd said she sent him train fare, but there hadn't been any mention of payment for his service.

Is it possible Calhoon is in love with Mary? She was fairly attractive and seemed nice enough for the most part. Women like her were often loud and bad tempered, but not Mary. He got up and went to Barnes' desk.

"Come with me. We're going to check on Calhoon. I want you to agree with whatever I say to him. I'll fill you in on the way."

* * *

When they arrived at the hospital they were directed to Calhoon's room. Constable Smith was sitting on a chair outside.

"How's he doing?" Hodgins asked. "When Riley returned he said the doctor was still examining him."

"Some busted ribs, cuts and bruises on his face. The doc wants to keep him for a bit, but said he'll live."

"Right. I'll need you to stay a bit longer, but I'll send someone to take over shortly."

Hodgins opened the door and entered, Barnes right behind him. A nurse stood beside the bed, checking on Calhoon's bandages. She started to leave but Hodgins asked her to stay.

Calhoon's face was completely wrapped giving him the appearance of a mummy. There were two small slits where his eyes were, and a small opening for his nostrils. The gauze went around his mouth allowing his two swollen lips to stick out. The sheet covered his body so Hodgins couldn't see if the rest of Calhoon was wrapped like his face.

"I'm gonna die, ain't I?" Calhoon asked. His speech was laboured and soft.

"Is there anything you want to get off your chest

before that happens?" Hodgins asked.

Calhoon said nothing.

Hodgins looked over at Barnes, who stood on the opposite side of the bed. Barnes started to say something, but Hodgins shook his head. Barnes nodded that he understood, but the confused look on his face was one Hodgins had seen many times.

Calhoon thinking he was dying changed Hodgins' plans slightly. Hodgins was certain Barnes would remember their earlier conversation and follow along without giving anything away. He turned his attention back to Calhoon.

"You're in love with Mary, aren't you?"

Calhoon turned his head slightly to look at Hodgins.

"That's why she didn't have to pay you to follow Nolan around."

"I'd do anything for her," Calhoon replied.

"But she's married to someone else. Why not kill him so you could have Mary all to yourself?"

"You don't understand."

"Why don't you explain it then?"

Calhoon turned to stare at the ceiling.

"She's my little sister."

"Your sister?" asked a shocked Barnes. "I don't see a family resemblance."

"*Half* sister."

"Well that explains why you didn't kill Nolan. I think I'm beginning to understand," Hodgins said. "You wanted your sister to be happy." He paused a moment. "You thought she'd be happy if Nolan's daughter was out of the way. That's why you killed her. An innocent girl."

"Mary's first husband was a lazy drunk. Violent too." Calhoon said. He winced and put a hand to his ribs, but kept talking.

"Gonna die anyway, so may as well admit what I dun. Going to Hell anyhow. Yah, I kilt the girl, and ya can't hang me fir it 'cause I'll already be dead."

Hodgins looked over at the nurse. "You heard his confession?"

She nodded.

"That's all I needed." He signalled to Barnes. "May as well go back to the station and write up the report."

Barnes was grinning ear to ear as they left.

"Very clever of you, Sir. He's going to be surprised when he finds out he's not actually dying."

Hodgins put his hand on Barnes' shoulder. "We're all going to die lad, eventually. He'll just be going out at the end of a rope."

* * *

"I'm glad you found out who murdered that poor child,"

Cordelia said as she settled into the settee. "I suppose in his mind he thought he was doing a good thing for his sister. I don't have any siblings, but I can't imagine actually killing someone just to make a sister happy."

"I love my brother, but I would never kill for him. Unless he was in danger of course. I would do anything to protect my family. If anyone ever hurt you or Sara, I don't even want to think what I would do to them."

"Well, now that that's over, I was thinking we should have a party to meet our new neighbours." She held up a hand. "Before you say no, I thought maybe towards the end of August we could have an afternoon lawn party. Nothing fancy. I've been so busy getting the house together I haven't been able to meet anyone properly, just a quick hello or wave.

"They could drop in any time during the afternoon. We can serve cold drinks and sandwiches. And maybe you can invite Constable Barnes and his family. I've noticed how fond you've become of him, and I'd love to meet his parents."

"I think that's a wonderful idea. I haven't met any of our neighbours, except for Halloway. And it would be nice to invite Henry and his family. He has a younger sister, same age as poor Olivia. She's older than Sara, but they might become friends."

Hodgins thought about Mr. Halloway and the constable, and smiled. "You know, Barnes seemed quite taken with their daughter, and Halloway was most impressed with Barnes. I'm sure Henry would like the chance to meet her. Who knows what might become of it?"

Cordelia laughed. "I never imagined you as a matchmaker Bertie. I've spoken to her very briefly, and she seems quite nice. Now you definitely have to invite him."

Hodgins sighed. "I wish I could invite my brother over. I haven't seen him since we wed. He's never even met his niece. And you're right about Henry. I think maybe I've sort of adopted him as a substitute brother. Always wanted a younger one. I'll write to my own and invite him and his family to visit with us. We have plenty of room now that we have our own place."

"That's a wonderful idea. You do that tonight and I'll post it first thing in the morning. Tomorrow Sara can help me make invitations for the party and hand deliver them. Then I'll make a list of everything we need to have ready before the party."

Hodgins smiled at the thought of seeing his brother again and went in search of some stationery.

ABOUT THE AUTHOR

Nanci M. Pattenden is a professional genealogist, and an author of historical crime fiction. Her interest in genealogy, local history and love of Victorian murder mysteries have merged to create a new Canadian Victorian murder mystery writer. She is a member of Crime Writers of Canada, The Writers Community of York Region, and the Ontario Genealogical Society.

She has completed the Creative Writing program at the University of Calgary, and has completed two programs with The Institute of Genealogical Studies (Canadian and English studies).

Nanci currently resides in Newmarket, Ontario.

nanci@nancipattenden.com
www.murderdoespayink.ca
www.nancipattenden.wordpress.com
@npattenden

CPSIA information can be obtained
at www.ICGtesting.com
Printed in the USA
LVHW011423050319
609546LV00004B/648/P

9 780991 897971